The Wages of Life

The Wages of Life

Vikram Kapur

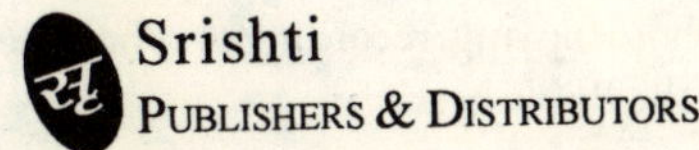

SRISHTI PUBLISHERS & DISTRIBUTORS
64-A, Adhchini
Sri Aurobindo Marg
New Delhi 110 017
srishtipublishers@yahoo.com

First published by SRISHTI PUBLISHERS & DISTRIBUTORS in 2004

ISBN 81-88575-30-5

Typeset in AGaramond 11pt. by Suresh Kumar Sharma at Srishti

Cover design: Shivani Babbar

Printed in India

For my father, Harbans Lal, with love

Acknowledgements

I am indebted to the following writers and books: Walter K. Anderson and Shridhar D. Damle, *The Brotherhood in Saffron: The Rashtriya Swayamsevak Sangh and Hindu Revivalism*; Pralay Kanungo, *RSS's Tryst with Politics*; Larry Collins and Dominique Lapierre, *Freedom at Midnight*; Prem Vaidya, *Savarkar: A Lifelong Crusader*. I am also indebted to Lawrence John and Santosh Pandey who were invaluable in the typing of the manuscript. And, above all, I am grateful to my family for their patience and encouragement, especially my father for sharing his memories of pre-partition Rawalpindi.

Vikram Kapur

Part One

One

On July 2, 2001, Ravi Malhotra, a computer engineer with Microsoft, returned from work to his apartment building in Seattle to find a blue aerogramme in his mailbox. He didn't have to turn it over to read the sender's name and address. From the handwriting on the front, he knew it was a letter from his father in Delhi.

He tucked it away with the rest of his mail in his trousers pockets and pressed the button for the elevator. He lived alone in a two-bedroom apartment on the second floor of the building. As he waited for the elevator, two boys, shrieking with laughter, burst through the front door of the building and headed straight for the stairs. A third followed close behind. Ravi listened to the three of them running up the stairs and wished he had just a bit of their energy. As it was, at the end of the day, he found it hard to drag himself up even one flight of stairs to his apartment. With a shake of the head, he contemplated his waist, where the shirt bulged noticeably, thanks to the beginnings of a paunch.

He was thirty-two years old. Close to six feet tall, he was cleanshaven, with skin the color of cardboard. He had short black hair, a sloping forehead, bushy eyebrows, black eyes and a long pointed nose. His lips were invariably pursed. What had begun as a conscious effort to compensate for a thin upper lip had, over the years, hardened into a habit. In the past year, the strain of staring at computer screens all day had also caught up with him, forcing him to wear glasses. Like many people new to wearing glasses, however, he chose to take his off whenever he could. Right now they rested in his trousers pockets. He was dressed in a pair of dark trousers, a long-sleeved blue shirt and brown leather shoes. The tie he had taken off soon after leaving his office. It now lay in the briefcase that he carried in his right hand.

He rode the elevator up and then emerged to make his way down a long corridor to his apartment. His apartment was at the end of the corridor. Presently, he reached the front door. He unlocked it and went in. Once he was inside, he placed his briefcase on a side table and settled on the living room sofa. Then he put on his glasses and began to read his father's letter.

He read it once. Then he started over to read it again. Even then, when he was finished, he sat still for several minutes, unable to believe what he had just read.

Six months ago, he had gone to Delhi with the express purpose of bringing his father back with him. His mother had just died. With her gone and him being an only child, there was no way he could leave his father in Delhi. His father was in his seventies. Actually, he was almost eighty. At that age, surely he couldn't stay on his own.

To his surprise, his father dismissed the idea of going to America outright. In no uncertain terms, he told Ravi he had no intention of moving to a foreign country. Ravi pressed him. But the old man simply refused to budge. Finally, Ravi tried emotional blackmail, asking his father to think of his mother. Wouldn't she have wanted them to be together once she was gone? To which his father replied, as far as he was concerned, Ravi was welcome to come home any time he wished.

Even after returning to the U.S., Ravi raised the issue in his letters to his father. His father, however, chose to ignore it completely. With the result, ultimately Ravi gave up on the idea.

But now right out of the blue …

Ravi sprang to his feet. His mind was racing. First thing tomorrow, he'd talk to his boss and put in a leave application. Then he needed to call the travel agent. He figured he could leave in a week to ten days, which gave him just enough time to do up the apartment for his father. Thankfully, it had two bedrooms. The first thing he needed to get for the other bedroom was a bed. Then, maybe a desk. Yes, definitely a desk. His father had been a journalist all his life. Even though he had given up his editorial position after his mother's death, he still wrote a weekly column for his newspaper. Furthermore, he read extensively. Come to think of it, an ashtray wouldn't be out of place with the desk. For, unlike him, his father was a smoker, and a pretty heavy one at that.

Then he wondered if it was a good idea to get too many things before he actually got his father. After all, he had to spend some time in India. With his father coming to live in the U.S., there would be plenty of things to take care of.

Whatever it was, he'd figure it out. The important thing was that his father was coming.

Whistling, he started to go to his bedroom to change into a pair of slippers. On the way, he passed his mother's picture hanging on the living room wall. He paused.

As per tradition, the picture wore the marigold garland of the deceased. It was seven years old, taken right after he was hired by Microsoft. In it his mother looked radiant, her face lit by the promise of a bright future for her son. These days, however, he ran into a completely different woman in his thoughts. A woman dying from tuberculosis that had eaten away her cheeks, sunk her eyes deep in their sockets and peeled so much flesh from her body that all that was left was bone.

His eyes grew misty and a lump entered his throat. For over a month before she had succumbed to the disease, it had been an effort for her even to speak. When they talked on the phone, she was often out of breath after a few words. And each time they spoke, the first thing she wanted to know was when he was coming home. Soon, he assured her, soon. Any day now his green card would be approved. His lawyer was confident. And then he'd be on his way to her. She only had to wait a little longer.

A long silence greeted his answer the last time they spoke. Then, in a cracked voice, she said she didn't think she had much time left.

Those were the last words she would ever say to him. The next day, he received the news of her death. As it turned out, he didn't even make it to her funeral. It was two weeks before his approval arrived and he could go to India.

Now, more than six months later, tears stung his eyes at the memory. He gazed at his father's letter that he still held in his hand. He had been unable to do anything for his mother in her old age. But now, at least, he had a chance with his father.

After changing into his slippers, Ravi made himself a cup of tea. By the time he was finished with the tea, it was six thirty. That would be seven tomorrow morning in Delhi, he calculated. Yes, his father would be up by now. He picked up the phone and dialed.

The servant Hari Singh answered the phone in Delhi. His father was having his morning tea in the garden. Ravi waited, while Hari Singh took the phone to him. He could see his father, still dressed in his kurta-pajama, seated in a cane chair in the middle of the garden. He'd be alternating sips of tea with drags from his first cigarette of the day, while examining the morning newspapers. Yes, *examining* was definitely the right word, for his father, like many newspapermen, reviewed rather than read newspapers. He started with the headlines and the pictures, before working his way into the articles, grimacing each time he saw a mistake.

"Ravi," it was his father's voice.

"Yes, Daddy, good morning."

"Good morning. What a wonderful surprise. How are you?"

"I'm fine, Daddy. I just got your letter and I can't tell you how happy I am that you're coming here. Just wish you had come six months ago."

There was a short pause. Then his father said, "I didn't say anything six months ago. But I was angry with you, Ravi. I thought you were selfish, putting your green card before your mother. So when you asked me to come and live with you, I had no hesitation in saying no. But now I am no longer angry."

He sighed.

"You know, Ravi, lately I've been doing a lot of looking back on my life," he said. "I guess the older we get the more we tend to do that, which isn't surprising as there is so much less to look forward to. And I have realized how little time I've spent being your father.

"You came as a miracle to us, Ravi. We had been married for fourteen years. We had practically given up all hope of ever having a child. And then there was you. When I held you in my arms for the first time, I wanted nothing more than to be a good father.

"But I couldn't do that. I was in my forties and I guess much too stuck in my ways. For too long my work had been my life. I could see the chief editor's chair waiting for me and I was determined to get it. Well, I got it all right, and I did a good job, too. But somewhere in there I forgot to be a good father.

"Your mother raised you, Ravi. I was just a bit player. You don't really know me, and I want to change that. Whatever time I have left I want to spend it with you, being your father."

Ravi swallowed. He was unable to speak. His eyes were brimming with tears that threatened to stream down his face.

"Ravi, are you still there?" his father asked.

Ravi wiped his eyes.

"Yes, Daddy, yes," he said.

He paused for an instant. Then he said, "Daddy."

"Yes, Ravi."

"If only Mummy could be with us."

He closed his eyes as he spoke. Tears, however, leaked out to form wet tracks down his face. He was forced to put the receiver down, as he tried to recover. It was several seconds before he could take it up again.

"Ravi, are you all right?" his father asked.

The old man's voice was choked.

"Yes, Daddy, I'm okay," Ravi said.

"There is nothing I could want more than to have your mother back," his father said. "When she was alive, I often took her for granted, I guess, because she was always there. Now that she's gone, I miss her terribly. I wish I could have told her how much she meant to me. But now it's too late. There is, however, still time for the two of us. And I intend to make good use of it. That's what your mother would want. You said so yourself, and you were right."

Two

Ravi recalled that conversation ten days later, as his plane touched down in Delhi close to midnight. Even after ten days, he couldn't get over the feeling and candor with which his father had spoken. He couldn't remember the last time his father had opened up to him like that. In fact, for as long as he could remember, his relationship with his father had been cordial, rather than intimate.

He had asked his father to come live with him out of a sense of duty, as well as a desire to atone for not being there for his mother. That conversation with his father, however, promised much more than that. It had all the makings of a new beginning for the two of them – one for which he was more than ready.

The last ten days had been hectic. What with buying his airline ticket and packing and taking care of things at the office and the apartment ... By the time he boarded the plane for Delhi, he was well and truly exhausted.

Now, however, after spending more than twenty hours en route, he felt very much alive. He couldn't wait to get off the plane and see his father. In his haste, he bumped the man in front of him and had to apologize.

He breezed through immigration and customs. Soon he was in the reception area for international arrivals. There he paused, leaning on his baggage cart, as he scanned the rows of faces clustered behind the railing for his father.

He didn't see him. However, he heard someone call out his name. He turned in the direction of the voice to spot Dr. Verma, one of his father's closest friends. He raised a hand in acknowledgement and made his way over.

Dr. Verma was a stocky man of five eight. In his seventies, he carried himself with the erect bearing of a much younger man. He had thin gray hair, a dome-shaped forehead and a gray moustache that tapered at the edges of his mouth. He wore glasses. That night he was dressed in gray trousers and a short-sleeved white shirt.

Ravi folded his hands and said namaste.

"How are you, Ravi?" Dr. Verma asked.

"I'm fine, Uncle," Ravi answered. "Have you seen Daddy anywhere? He was supposed to come and pick me up."

Dr. Verma hesitated. Then he said, "Your father couldn't come, Ravi. I've come in his place."

"He couldn't come? Why? Is he okay?"

Dr. Verma put his arm round Ravi's back.

"Come on, son," he said. "Let's get out of here. I will tell you everything on the way."

His chauffeur was waiting outside with the car. He placed Ravi's bags in the trunk. Then they were underway. Ravi, seated in the back of the car with Dr. Verma, felt the clammy hands of fear running all over him. His gut told him something terrible had happened.

"Ravi," Dr. Verma said, finally. "I'm afraid I have some very bad news for you.

"This evening your father met with an accident. He was out walking and he was hit by a car. He was rushed to the hospital. There the doctors did their best. But they could not save him."

Ravi remembered little of the rest of that night. He was in complete shock.

Instead of taking him home, Dr. Verma took him to his own house, where he gave him a sedative with a cup of tea. Within minutes, Ravi was asleep.

When he woke up, it was morning. He was lying in a bed in a room with blue walls and a white ceiling. He was still dressed in his shirt and trousers. His shoes and socks, however, were on the floor beside the bed.

He lay awake, trying to figure out where he was. Then he remembered.

Last night the news of his father's death had hit him with

the force of a punch dropping someone unconscious to the floor. Today, however, things were different. It was as if he had woken up from a coma. Part of him craved to sink back into it, for now he could feel and all there was to feel was pain.

Tears swelled out of his eyes. For a while, he was content to simply lie there and let them flow. Even after they dried up, he continued to lie still with his hands clasped behind the back of his head.

He had lived on his own in another country for the better part of the last seven years. At no point in his life, however, had he felt more alone.

With both his parents gone, he had no one he could call family. His parents, like him, had been only children. His father was a refugee who had fled, what was now Pakistan, for Delhi when India was partitioned in 1947. All his father's relatives, including his parents, had been killed in the riots accompanying partition. His mother would have been a refugee as well, if her father hadn't gotten a job in Delhi in 1945. Her extended family, however, had been in the part of India that had gone to Pakistan during partition. The riots had consumed them as well.

With the result, he had grown up without any aunts, uncles or cousins. The only family he had known, other than his parents, were his maternal grandparents who were long dead.

His mother had often pointed to this paucity of relatives as a reason why he should marry. "Your father and I are not getting any younger," she would say. "And other than us you have no one in the world. So the sooner you get married the better it is. At least then you won't be on your own." Her sense of urgency, however, was lost on him. He could see nothing wrong with her or his father. Furthermore, he had his career to think of. The way he saw it, here he was struggling to establish himself in a foreign country, and she wanted to saddle him with a wife! "What's the big hurry?" he said to his mother. "At least wait until I get my green card." To which his mother replied, "You may think you have all the time in the world, Ravi. But before you know it, it can run out and leave you ruing the fact that you waited so long."

Which was exactly what had happened. Nine months ago, she had been diagnosed with tuberculosis. In less than three months, she was dead. And now, a little more than six months later, so was his father.

"Ravi."

Dr. Verma's voice startled him. He sat up to see him standing near the foot of the bed. He was dressed in a cream-colored kurta-pajama. Ravi had been so immersed in his own thoughts that he hadn't heard him come into the room.

"I knocked a few times," Dr. Verma said. "But there was no answer. So I came in to see if you were still sleeping."

"I'm sorry, Uncle," Ravi said. "I just didn't hear you."

There was a tremor in his voice. Dr. Verma sat down on the edge of the bed.

"I was your age when I lost my parents," he said. "So I know how you feel."

"You never think your parents are going to die, do you?" Ravi said. "You think they'll live forever. So you take them for granted. Other things become more urgent –career, ambition, money … You always think you'll have time for your parents later, when you've got everything you ever wanted. And then one day you wake up and you find that they are gone and all you have left are memories and regrets."

Dr. Verma put his hand on Ravi's shoulder.

"You have to get a hold on yourself, son," he said. "At times like these it is very easy to go to pieces. Nothing seems worth it. Even the simplest task requires an effort. This is when you must dig deep. You are a young man. You have a long life in front of you. You can't allow despair to overwhelm you. You have to fight it."

He rose to his feet.

"Come on," he said. "Your aunty has breakfast ready downstairs. You didn't eat anything last night. You must have some."

Though he wasn't hungry, Ravi climbed out of bed and accompanied Dr. Verma downstairs. All he could manage at the breakfast table, however, was a slice of toast with his tea. After breakfast, Dr. Verma asked him to join him in the drawing room. The drawing room was adjacent to the dining room. As Ravi settled in one of its overstuffed chairs, his eyes fell on that day's edition of *The Indian Republic*, lying on a peg table beside the chair. On the front page, dominated by the Pakistani President Pervez Musharraf's forthcoming visit to India that weekend, there was a story about his father's death in the column to the extreme right. It had a picture of his father. Above the picture was a headline that read: ASHISH MALHOTRA, FORMER EDITOR-IN-CHIEF AND COLUMNIST OF THE REPUBLIC, KILLED IN A ROAD ACCIDENT.

Ravi stared at the headline. He had just remembered something that Dr. Verma had told him last night.

"Uncle, you said last night that Daddy was out walking when he was hit by that car," he said.

"Yes," Dr. Verma said.

"What time was it?"

"About six."

"When I landed last night the temperature was touching thirty-five. At six'o clock it would have been close to forty. What was Daddy doing out walking in that heat?"

Dr. Verma shook his head.

"What's more, Daddy never walked anywhere," Ravi continued. "Not if he could help it. The Basant Lok shopping complex is barely a ten-minute walk from our house. When I was a kid, Daddy would often take me there for a treat at Nirula's. Given how bad traffic got in front of Basant Lok and the atrocious parking situation, it made much more sense to walk there. But even in winter, when it was cool and pleasant,

Daddy refused to walk. At times I actually wanted to and he insisted on taking the car. Yet, yesterday, at the height of summer, with an air-conditioned, chauffeur-driven car sitting in his garage, he chose to walk. Why?"

"Maybe he was just going somewhere close by," Dr. Verma said. "To meet a neighbor or maybe buy something from that market near your house."

'Well, all the neighbors we used to know are either dead or have moved away. Their houses have been torn down and flats have come up in their place. The people who live in these flats are either young corporate executives or foreign diplomats posted in India. I don't think my father would know any of them. He certainly did not, when I was here six months ago. And as for buying something from D-block market is concerned, for that he could have sent one of the servants. He didn't have to go himself."

"Maybe there was something wrong with the car then?"

"Maybe. Where did the accident happen?"

"On Poorvi Marg, close to where it intersects Paschimi Marg."

"That intersection can't be more than two hundred yards from our house. "

"Yes."

"What about the car that hit him?"

"It simply drove away. Your father was left lying on the road.

He was unconscious and bleeding badly. Atma Ram ..."

"Atma Ram?" Ravi interrupted.

"Yes, he's a fruit seller."

"I know who he is. He has his shop by the road near that intersection. He's been there for almost twenty years. My mother used to buy fruit from him. He'd even deliver it to our house."

"Atma Ram was at his shop when it happened. He rushed to the spot with a few other men and recognized your father. They flagged down a passing car to take him to the hospital. Then Atma Ram went to your house and told Hari Singh what had happened. Hari Singh promptly called me on my mobile. Just a few weeks back your father had given him that number to call in the event of an emergency."

Ravi was quiet for a moment, reflecting on what Dr. Verma had just said.

"I'm sorry, Uncle," he said, finally, "but I don't understand. As far as I can recall, Dr. Uppal was my father's doctor. Then why did he give Hari Singh your number to call in the case of an emergency? Furthermore, you are a cardiologist!"

Dr. Verma took a deep breath.

"I promised your father I wouldn't breathe a word of it to you," he said. "He wanted to tell you himself when the time was right. But now I don't think it makes a difference.

"About four weeks ago your father came to me complaining

of chest pains. I ran some tests on him and discovered he had lung cancer."

"What?" Ravi said.

"I wish he had listened to me. So many times I told him to cut down on his smoking, if not quit altogether. But he wouldn't listen. I ran the tests twice to make sure. There was no mistake. It was cancer all right and at a fairly advanced stage. I didn't think he had more than a year to live."

Ravi stared at him. The knowledge that he could be dead within a year had prompted his father to change his mind about living with him in America. He could see that now.

The realization, however, gave him little comfort. A year! Right now he'd give his right arm for one more day with his father.

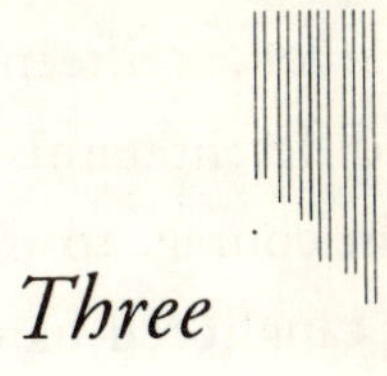

Three

At lunch, Ravi told Dr. Verma that he wanted to go home. Dr. Verma tried to persuade him to stay a little longer. But Ravi had made up his mind. As much as he found the prospect of being alone in his own house daunting, he felt he couldn't very well avail of Dr. Verma's hospitality any longer.

They left soon after lunch. It was a thirty-minute drive from Dr. Verma's house in Golf Links to Ravi's house in Vasant Vihar. In the beginning, Dr. Verma attempted to make small talk. Soon, however, he figured out that Ravi didn't have the heart for it. So he fell silent as well.

As the road wound southward towards Vasant Vihar, it took them past several places that had been a part of Ravi's youth. There was the Junior Modern School on Humayun Road, where he had studied until class five. There was the Delhi Gymkhana Club, across the street from the racecourse, where he had spent countless afternoons playing tennis as a boy. There was the Nehru Park in Chanakya Puri, where he had gone on school picnics ... As Ravi watched them drift past, a host of bittersweet memories surfaced from the depths of his mind. He saw himself at eight, at ten, at fifteen ... He was a prankster, an enthusiastically indifferent tennis player, a would-be lover trying to screw up the courage to ask a girl to a movie ... He saw himself getting caught red-handed in a prank and facing the wrath of the teacher, huffing and puffing on the tennis court as his shots continued to find the net, wondering why the words he had practiced saying a million times in front of the bathroom mirror slipped completely from his mind when he came face to face with the girl ...

It was a comfort to see the old places again. After losing both his parents within a year, it was a relief to know that some of what he had known growing up was still standing.

Finally, the car made a right on to Poorvi Marg. Unease clawed at Ravi's stomach. He was in his own neighborhood. Within minutes, he'd be home. Despite the airconditioning in the car, he began to sweat. His hands were clenched, his eyes furtive ... He wanted to tell the chauffeur to turn the car around. He wasn't ready to go home just yet. The wound was far too fresh ...

He felt Dr. Verma's hand on his arm.

"Are you all right?" Dr. Verma asked.

Ravi swallowed.

"Yes," he said.

The car stopped in front of his house – number 40. Bahadur, the Gurkha security guard, saluted and opened the gate. In less than a minute, they were in the driveway, standing outside the front door.

Dr. Verma stayed for a cup of tea. Then he rose to leave. Ravi saw him off at the front door, promising to call if he needed something.

Hari Singh lingered, asking Ravi if he wanted more tea. Ravi hesitated. He didn't really want any more. But he didn't wish to be alone just yet either, which he would be if he dismissed Hari Singh. So he told him to get a cup.

While Hari Singh got the tea, Ravi settled on the sofa in the drawing room. It was a large drawing room, about sixteen by fourteen feet. Other than the sofa, it had a divan, a loveseat, four overstuffed chairs and a fully equipped entertainment center. A Persian carpet, with floral designs embroidered in bright colors against a yellow background, covered the floor. Side tables were placed next to the chair, loveseat and sofa, while a round mahogany table stood in the middle of the room.

Besides the drawing room, the house had a dining room, a kitchen and four bedrooms with attached bathrooms. There was also a garden out front. The driveway ran straight beside the garden and the house. Therefore, the front door was actually a side door. At the end of the driveway, there was a garage with the servant quarters built on top. And the entire compound, all eight hundred square yards of it, was enclosed within a ten-foot high boundary wall.

Given its size, the house kept the cleaning lady busy for at least two hours every morning. One time, when Ravi was a schoolboy, they were between cleaning ladies. With the result, the entire responsibility for cleaning the house fell on his mother. Watching her slave away, Ravi wondered aloud why she and his father had constructed such a monster of a house. Since it was only the three of them, it wasn't as if they needed the space. To which his mother answered, "But it won't always be like this. You will grow up, get married and have children. Then this house will be full."

As it turned out, now the house was emptier than ever before.

Hari Singh returned with the tea. Ravi asked him to stay while he drank it. Hari Singh stood about, looking nonplussed, apparently taken aback by the request. Finally, he put the tray down on the mahogany table and sat down crosslegged on the carpet in front of Ravi.

He was round Ravi's age and build. His wife and two children, to whom he sent money every month, still lived in his village in Haryana with his parents. He had been with Ravi's family for the last six years, doubling as the houseboy and the cook. That day he was dressed in a white T-shirt and a pair of blue trousers that had once belonged to Ravi. Ravi recognized the pair as one he had discarded years ago. His mother must have given it to Hari Singh.

Hari Singh had already conveyed his condolences to Ravi, as had the other two servants present – Bahadur the security guard and Suresh the chauffeur. Now he appeared anxious, fidgeting as he sat there on the carpet. Ravi immediately regretted asking him to stay. He could see, in his desire for company, he had inadvertently caused consternation. From Hari Singh's perspective, the fact the master had told him to stick around, instead of dismissing him, could only mean the master had something to say to him, possibly something unwelcome. For masters never asked servants to stay for their company.

Ravi hastened to put him at ease.

"This is very good tea," he said.

No sooner than he spoke, he realized he hadn't even tasted it. Quickly, he took a sip and nodded approvingly at Hari Singh.

"You are very kind, sahib," Hari Singh said.

There was silence, as Ravi found himself at a complete loss as to what to say to Hari Singh. Although they were both north Indians and round the same age, the difference in class left them with very little in common.

"Has it been this hot all month?" he asked, finally.

"Yes, sahib. It's been like this since May."

Again, there was silence. Ravi sipped his tea. He had exhausted the weather. What next? Then he remembered that

Hari Singh was the cook.

"Do you have enough food in the house?" he asked.

"Yes, sahib. There are vegetables, dal ... The only thing that's finished is the fruit. But I can go get it from Atma Ram. It will only take a few minutes."

The mention of Atma Ram's name reminded Ravi of his conversation with Dr. Verma in the morning.

"Atma Ram was the one who came and told you about my father's accident," he said to Hari Singh.

"Yes, sahib."

"Tell me, was there something wrong with the car yesterday that my father had to go out walking?"

"No, sahib. Actually, when your father told me he was going out, I was going to tell Suresh to get the car out. But your father stopped me. He said he didn't need the car."

That was strange.

"Do you know why my father went out?"

"No, sahib. Actually, he took me by surprise when he said he was going out. He was home all morning and afternoon. Even at five'o clock, there was no sign he was planning to go out. In fact, a little after five yesterday, he called me and told me to give him his tea early. He wanted me to go to the sweetshop in A-block market. You were coming at night and he wanted me to get all your favorite sweets. A-block market is a few kilometers away. It would have taken me a while to go there and come back. So he reckoned it was better if I served the tea right then before I left."

"Then what happened?"

"I started making the tea. He went to the bathroom. While he was inside, the phone rang. I picked it up. It was a madam. She wanted to talk to him. I told her he was in the bathroom and took down her name and phone number."

"Who was she?"

"She said she was Miss Sapna Sood from Jawaharlal Nehru University."

Ravi didn't recognize the name.

'Did she tell you why she wanted to talk to my father?"

"No, sahib."

"Did my father call her back?"

"Yes, sahib. Right after he returned from the bathroom."

"What did he talk to her about?"

"I don't know, sahib. I went back to the kitchen to finish making the tea. By the time I came out again, he was finished with the phone call. However, he was still standing by the phone. He appeared to be deep in thought. I told him that tea was ready. He said he was going out and would have it once he got back. I asked if he wanted me to go get the sweets now or wait for him to return. 'What sweets?' he said. Then he remembered. He said I could go when he got back."

Clearly, his father had no intention of going out yesterday evening. Something, however, had happened during that phone call with Sapna Sood that changed his mind. What?

'You said you wrote down this Sapna Sood's phone number," Ravi said. "Where?"

"In the pad next to the telephone."

Four

The telephone number, Hari Singh had written down for Sapna Sood, turned out to be the telephone number of the history department of Jawaharlal Nehru University. Sapna Sood was a research scholar working towards her Ph.D. She wasn't in when Ravi called. Ravi left his name and telephone number with the secretary. After living in the U.S., it felt strange to deal with a male secretary.

After ringing off, Ravi decided to go and talk to Atma Ram. He wanted to know exactly how the accident had taken place.

Atma Ram's shop was less than two hundred yards from the house. For Ravi, however, getting there proved more challenging than walking many a mile. No longer used to the Delhi summer, he found the stuffy afternoon air trying, to say the least. Add to that the mosquitoes and the hot sun … He was in some discomfort as he made his way up Poorvi Marg, with an increasingly wet handkerchief crushed in his palm.

Newly constructed multi-storied flats and the few independent houses that were still surviving lined both sides of the street to his right and left. After 28 Poorvi Marg, the line to his left ended and there was a gap in the pavement that acted as the entrance to the D-block market parking lot. Atma Ram's shop was located just before this gap. It was at the edge of the pavement, under a tarpaulin roof held up by wooden poles. About ten yards further down, Poorvi Marg and Paschimi Marg met.

Atma Ram was sitting inside his shop. He had taken his shirt off due to the heat. When he saw Ravi, however, he promptly put it back on and told his fifteen-year-old son, who worked for him, to go get Ravi a Coke. The last thing Ravi wanted after two cups of tea was a Coke. However, he kept quiet, knowing Atma Ram would be hurt if he refused the Coke.

Atma Ram was a short, stocky man in his mid-forties. He had lost some hair since Ravi had seen him last; he now had a bald spot in the middle of his head. The hair he had left was graying as well. His moustache, however, was still jet black and as luxuriant as ever.

He gave Ravi his own chair and settled on the stool on which his son had been sitting. Ravi sighed, glad to duck out of the sun under the tarpaulin.

"I am very sorry about your father, sahib," Atma Ram said. "I guess one can't change what's written in one's fate. But when it happens in such a way ..."

He shook his head.

"You saw the accident happen," Ravi said.

"Yes, sahib. It happened right here. Your father was on his

way home from the market. He had just walked across the parking lot and was about to come out on to the road when the car hit him."

So his father had gone to the market. Why?

"Do you know where my father went in the market?" he asked Atma Ram.

'Yes, sahib. He went to the public telephone booth."

"The public telephone booth?"

"Yes, sahib. He passed here about five thirty, maybe a few minutes before that. I don't remember the exact time. But I know it was before I went for my chai. I usually go around five thirty.

"A few minutes after he passed by, I left my son in charge of the shop and went to get some chai. The chai shop is right by the public telephone booth. As I drank my chai, I could see him there, waiting his turn. I was at the chai shop for ten to fifteen minutes. Then I came back to my shop. Before I left the chai shop, however, I remember seeing him going into the booth."

Ravi stared at Atma Ram. His father had left the house to get in line to make a call from the public telephone booth. That explained why he had walked. He didn't want the chauffeur wondering whether he was a little crazy, going to use the public telephone when there was a perfectly good phone in thehouse. Furthermore, the very fact he had chosen to use the public telephone meant he wanted to keep the conversation a secret.

As a journalist, his father had often preferred public telephones to his home phone, especially after Emergency was declared in 1975. During the Emergency, the freedom of the press was curtailed and phones of journalists wiretapped. Such a situation existed for two years, until the Emergency was lifted in 1977 and full democratic freedoms restored. The whole experience, however, left his father distrustful of phones. With the result, even after 1977, he continued to use public telephones whenever he was working on something sensitive.

But what could be so sensitive that he had to use the public telephone yesterday? Just the day before, he had retired from his newspaper. So it couldn't be anything related to his work.

What could Sapna Sood have said to him that prompted him to go out and use the public telephone?

Atma Ram's son returned with the Coke. Ravi sipped it in silence. Then, after a short pause, he said to Atma Ram, "You said you saw my father enter the public telephone booth before you came back to your shop. Then when did you see him?"

"Five, maybe ten minutes after I reached my shop. He was just passing by here on his way home."

"That was when the car hit him."

"Yes, sahib."

"You said he was just about to step on to the road when he got hit. So you mean he was just coming out of the parking lot?"

"Yes, sahib."

"Was the car turning in to park?"

"No, sahib, the car came out of the parking lot."

"Came out of the parking lot?"

"Yes, sahib. He got hit from behind. He didn't have a chance."

"And the driver just drove away."

"Yes, sahib. He didn't wait for a second. Before any of us could do anything, he was gone. I rushed to your father. He was unconscious and bleeding badly. Me and a couple of other men stopped a passing car and sent him to the hospital. Then I went to your house. Later that evening I even went to the temple to pray for him. But …"

He looked down.

"Did you see who was driving the car that hit him?" Ravi asked.

"No, sahib. The car had dark windows."

"What kind of car was it?"

"It was a white Ambassador."

"What was its license plate number?"

"I didn't see it."

"What? But the car passed right here."

"Yes, sahib, it did. But the license plates were covered."

"Covered?"

"Yes, sahib. There was a black covering on them, both on

the front and the back. Also, sahib …"

He glanced to his right and left, then leaned forward.

"About three'o clock yesterday afternoon," he said in a low voice, "I went to deliver some fruit to a flat in number 41. As I passed your house, I noticed a white Ambassador standing in the bylane across the street. I am sure it was the same car, because that one, too, had a black covering over its license plates."

His father hadn't died in an accident. He had been deliberately murdered.

Everything Atma Ram had just told him pointed to that. The covered license plates, the speed with which the driver escaped, the car's dark windows . . . But more than anything, it was the fact the car had been lying in wait in the bylane in front of the house.

There was no doubt the car Atma Ram had seen at three in the afternoon was the same car that killed his father. In an upscale South Delhi neighborhood like Vasant Vihar, Ambassadors were rare. They had long been replaced by the trendier Marutis, Hondas and BMWs. The very idea that there could be two Ambassadors, both white and with covered license plates, in the vicinity of his house in the space of a few hours was a bit hard to swallow.

The Ambassador could have been standing in that bylane well before Atma Ram saw it. From there you got a clear view of the front of the house. So whoever was in that car would have seen his father come out of the front gate. After coming out of the gate, his father would have walked on the pavement from the house to Atma Ram's shop. The Ambassador would have followed, biding its time. It could have run him over when he stepped off the pavement at the entrance to the D-block market parking lot. But then the driver would have had to back his car to make his escape. So he decided, instead, to wait in the parking lot and get him on the way back.

"Sahib, your Coke is getting warm," Atma Ram's son said, cutting into his thoughts.

Atma Ram was busy with a customer. Ravi gulped the rest of his Coke down and said goodbye. Emerging from under the tarpaulin, he turned left towards D-block market.

The market itself was nothing more than three small, gray-colored buildings. Two of them, that had three stories each, stood with their backs to each other, while the third, a squat, two-story building, nestled on one side. All the shops were located towards the front of the building that was at the back of the one facing the parking lot. The building, facing the parking lot, as well as the two-story building to its right, contained only offices. At that time, the parking lot was full. At the time his father was killed, however, it was generally deserted, as the offices closed at five. The people frequenting the shops didn't park in that parking lot; they preferred the one on the other side, which was right in front of the shops.

The parking lot wasn't large; actually, it was no more than

fifteen yards straight and across. An Ambassador wasn't known for its pickup. However, it was a heavy car and his father had been on foot. Moreover, the last thing his father would have been expecting was to be hit in the back by a car. So even if it weren't going at full tilt, it would still have been capable of delivering a fatal blow. And once it was out of the parking lot, it would find plenty of clear road to crank up to full speed and make a swift escape. These were, after all, suburban streets, rather than major thoroughfares crammed with traffic.

Ravi stayed in the parking lot for a few more minutes. Then he made his way home. By the time he reached his house, he was sweaty all over. He flopped on a chair that was directly under the ceiling fan and told Hari Singh to get him a glass of water. When Hari Singh came back with the water, Ravi held the cool surface of the glass against his forehead for a few seconds before drinking up.

After returning the empty glass to Hari Singh, he sat still, staring into the distance.

All this while, he had been crushed by his father's loss. Now, however, he felt something completely different – a smoldering anger.

Whatever else he did, he had to find his father's murderer.

Five

Ravi called Hari Singh and asked him if anyone from the police had come by, with regard to his father's accident. Hari Singh said an Assistant Sub-Inspector or A.S.I. by the name of Kapil had stopped by last evening. He had got the address from Atma Ram, while taking down his eyewitness account. Hari Singh had told the A.S.I. that Ravi was coming from America later that night. The A.S.I. had taken down the phone number and said he'd call in the morning. He hadn't called so far.

Ravi dismissed Hari Singh. Then he rang up the Vasant Vihar police station and asked to speak to A.S.I. Kapil. The head constable on duty informed him that Kapil was gone for the day; he worked from eight to four and now it was close to five. Ravi was surprised. If Kapil got off at four, then how come he was out investigating something that had happened round six'o clock yesterday evening.

However, he kept his surprise to himself. After telling the head constable who he was, he said he really needed to speak to the A.S.I. as soon as possible about his father's case; so if, somehow, the head constable could help him get hold of

Kapil today, he'd be grateful. The head constable told him there was no need to talk to Kapil, since the case had been reassigned to A.S.I. Rawat. Rawat, however, was out sick. Now Ravi was well and truly foxed. If Kapil had begun the investigation, then why had the case been taken away from him in less than a day? He asked to speak to the Station House Officer or the S.H.O. in charge of the police station. He was told the S.H.O., whose name was Puri, wasn't in as well. In fact, he hadn't been in all day. He had married his daughter off the night before and would only return on Monday. Ravi lost his patience. Practically shouting, he demanded to know if there was anyone at all who could help him. The head constable said it was best if he called back after the weekend. With the Pakistani President in town tomorrow, the entire police force had their hands full ensuring his security that weekend.

Ravi banged the phone down in his frustration. It was a few minutes before he was calm again. Once he recovered his composure, he called the history department of Jawaharlal Nehru University and asked for Sapna Sood. The secretary told him she hadn't been back all afternoon. He very much doubted whether she'd be back today and suggested that Ravi try back on Monday. Ravi sighed. Before signing off, however, he requested the secretary to mark the message urgent, nevertheless.

Hari Singh came in with the day's mail. It was mostly junk.

There was, however, a manila envelope in his father's name that had come from *The Indian Republic*. Ravi opened the envelope to find a note, attached with a paper clip, to a newspaper clipping. He fished in his trousers pockets for his glasses. After putting them on, he looked at the note.

It was signed Rashmi. From the honorific salutation – Respected Sir – Ravi concluded that Rashmi was a junior reporter with *The Republic*. Her note read: Here is what you wanted.

Ravi glanced at the clipping. It had the byline – Rashmi Menon. It was a Page 10 story from the February 20, 1999, edition of the newspaper about a protest against Prime Minister Atal Bihari Vajpayee's peace mission to Pakistan. There was a picture of five protesters, belonging to a group he had never heard of called the Hindu Tigers, holding placards that read SHAME ON YOU VAJPAYEE and PAKISTANIS ONLY LEARN FROM KICKS.

The postal stamp, on the outside of the envelope, indicated it had been mailed yesterday. Why had his father wanted a story, more than two years old, about a few people protesting the Prime Minister's trip to Pakistan? If memory served him right, that peace mission had come to naught, as a few months later India and Pakistan found themselves fighting a war in Kargil.

He decided to talk to Rashmi. Journalists generally stayed in the newsroom until late in the evening. Well, at least they had in his father's day. He was glad to learn the trend hadn't changed. Within a minute, after he called *The Republic*, he had Rashmi on the line.

He started out by introducing himself, after which they talked about his father for a few minutes. Ravi learned that his father had hired Rashmi when he was editor-in-chief. From the glowing, almost worshipful way she spoke about him, he had evidently acted as her mentor as well.

Finally, Ravi got round to asking her about the clipping.

"Yes, I sent it yesterday," Rashmi said. "Your father called in the morning and asked for it."

"Did he tell you why he wanted it?"

"No."

Nor would she have inquired. She was, after all, a junior being requested a favor by a revered mentor to whom she owed her job.

"I did wonder about it, though," she said. "It was strange that he should ask for a story that I did more than two years ago the day after he retired – that too a story involving an obscure Hindu radical group. But then he had acted strangely the day before, too."

"Acted strangely? What do you mean?"

"Well, I had just bought a book from a secondhand bookstore close to where I live. I had been so busy, however, that I hadn't had the time to start reading it. So two days ago

I brought it to the office, thinking maybe I'd read it during my lunch break. It was lying on top of my desk.

"About eleven thirty your father came to my cubicle. It was his last day at the paper. He was saying goodbye to everybody. I had just done a feature on the many years he had spent at *The Republic* and his contribution to the newspaper. It had run in that morning's edition to coincide with his retirement. I was anxious to learn what he thought of it. After all he had done for me, the last thing I wanted was to displease him.

"So I was pretty nervous when he came in. He, however, put me at ease immediately by telling me how much he liked it. While we were talking, my phone rang. I excused myself to answer it. While I was on the phone, he began to browse through the book lying on my desk. I was on the phone for a few minutes. By the time I got off, his mood had changed completely.

"He had the book open and was staring at it. He looked as if he had just seen a ghost. His eyes were opened wide. Even his mouth was open.

"I asked him what had happened. I don't think he heard me the first time. When I repeated the question, he looked up and asked me where I got the book. I said I found it in a secondhand bookstore near my flat. He wanted to know the name of the bookstore. I couldn't remember it off the top of my head. He lost patience and shouted at me, asking what kind of reporter I was if I couldn't recall names. I was pretty disturbed by his outburst. He had never shouted at me before. Quickly, I wrote down the name and exact location of the bookstore on a piece of paper. He wanted to know if he could keep the book for a few days. I told him he could have it for as long as he wished.

"I was pretty upset for the rest of the day. The next morning, however, when he called to ask for the story, he apologized. That made me feel better."

It certainly wasn't in his father's nature to lose his cool in the way she had described. That, too, over a book.

"What book was this?" he asked her.

"*The Case of the Dangerous Dowager* by Erle Stanley Gardner. It's a Perry Mason novel."

A black and white image of Raymond Burr as Perry Mason on American television flashed in Ravi's mind. His father and Perry Mason! That was one odd couple. For that matter, his father's interest in a novel was surprising in itself. He rarely, if ever, read fiction.

"What's the name of the bookstore where you got the book?" Ravi asked Rashmi.

"It's called the Popular Book Depot," she said. "It's in R.K. Puram."

She had nothing more to tell him. So they said goodbye. For the next few minutes, Ravi re-ran the conversation in his mind. Then he shook his head. None of it made any sense.

The phone rang. It was Sapna Sood.

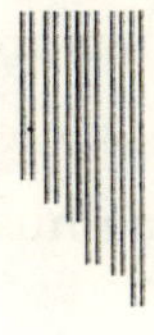

Six

Sapna Sood suggested they meet tomorrow. Ravi, she said, must have had a traumatic day. Then she still had some work to finish and it would soon begin getting dark, anyway. Ravi, however, told her he really needed to see her that evening. He said he was prepared to meet her wherever she wanted. Finally, she told him to come to the Basant Lok shopping complex in forty-five minutes. Since Basant Lok was halfway between Ravi's house and Jawaharlal Nehru University, it would be convenient for both of them. She asked him to come to the newsstand in front of the McDonald's.

Ravi arrived early. In order to kill time, he walked about. Basant Lok today looked very different to the one he had known growing up. Many of its old mainstays had disappeared. Those that still remained had changed character completely. The Priya cinema was now a multiplex. The Nirula's fast-food restaurant had been evicted from its pre-eminent location and now languished towards the back of the complex. Only the Modern Bazaar grocery store still appeared the same. After spending a few minutes inside, however, Ravi realized that, too, was an illusion. Gone was the tribe of homely, pleasantly-plump housewives who would spend hours browsing its wares. Today's shoppers were lean working women, who bought things off shopping lists, while juggling husbands, children and clients on the cellphone.

The biggest change, however, was manifested by the armada of multinationals that had sailed in. Other than the McDonald's, a Pizza Hut and a TGIF vied for a share of the consumer's stomach. A Nike store squared off with an Adidas store in a back-to- back duel for the feet, while a melange of pretty faces, drawn from all over the world, beamed from a Benetton sign to entice people into buying clothes ... There were also many more people around than Ravi could remember. For the most part, they were teenagers and young adults. That much, at least, hadn't changed; Basant Lok remained a magnet for the city's young. Today's young, however, behaved in ways unheard of when Ravi was their age. They greeted each other with hugs and kisses. The girls wore shorts and sleeveless T-shirts and smoked cigarettes in public without a care in the world ... To Ravi it all simply underlined the fact that he belonged to another generation, one that was no longer young or hip.

He glanced at his watch and made his way to the newsstand. A little later, he felt a tap on his shoulder.

"You must be Ravi Malhotra," the woman said. "Hi, I'm Sapna Sood."

(Later, when he asked her how she had placed him among

so many people, despite never having seen him before, she simply raised her eyebrows and said, "Who else would be standing about looking so lost except a Non Resident Indian?")

She was a slim, fair woman of five eight, dressed in a pair of jeans and a white T-shirt. A black handbag dangled from her right shoulder. She had an oval face, framed by straight black hair that flowed down her shoulders to the middle of her back. Her eyes were brown, her mouth full and wide. She had a long thin nose that curved upward near the tip. Ravi guessed she was in her late twenties. He wasn't far wrong. She had just turned thirty.

She had been doing research in the library all day. Consequently, she had missed lunch. She suggested they go to the McDonald's. He wasn't hungry. However, he agreed to go along with her.

At the McDonald's, while she waited her turn at the cash register, Ravi went looking for a table in the seating area upstairs. The place was full. It was a few minutes before he finally got a table.

A family of three was seated at the table adjoining his. The son, who must have been in his late teens or early twenties, was talking animatedly. Having just aced his college exams, he was mapping out his plans for the future, while his parents gazed fondly from the other side of the table. Ravi listened to his exuberant voice, detailing triumph after triumph with a conviction possible only in the unknowing enthusiasm of youth. It didn't seem that long ago when he was that young man. And now here he was, after losing both his parents, feeling his way about with the sureness of a blind man.

Some of what he felt must have showed on his face. For he sensed a hand on his shoulder and looked up to see Sapna Sood eyeing him with concern.

"We can do this some other day," she said.

"No, it's okay."

"Are you sure?"

"Yes."

He tried to smile. She offered him tea. He took a few sips from the paper cup, after which he felt better.

He could sense her waiting for him. On the phone, he had told her he needed to talk to her about his father. He had given the distinct impression he had something to tell her. The fact, she had agreed to meet him at all today, indicated he had hit the right chord. He didn't think she'd be seeing him, if he had said he had a bunch of questions for her.

He decided to plunge ahead.

"Miss Sood," he began.

"Sapna," she said.

"Sapna, you called my father yesterday."

She nodded.

"After talking to you yesterday, my father went out to make a call from the public telephone booth," he said. "That was something he used to do when he was working on something sensitive as a journalist. He simply didn't trust his home phone after it was tapped during the Emergency. But yesterday he wasn't working as a journalist. Something happened during your phone call that made him go out to the public telephone booth. What was it?"

She didn't answer. Ravi leaned forward.

"Sapna," he said, "my father was hit by that car when he was on his way back from the public telephone booth. If you hadn't called he wouldn't have gone there. And he'd still be alive today."

She puckered her lips. Then she reached inside her handbag and took out a picture that she handed to him.

It was a fading black and white shot. The backdrop appeared to be the inside of a shed. In the lower right-hand corner, one half of a teleprinter had squeezed its way into the shot. It was the three men, standing in the foreground, however, who commanded Ravi's attention. The one to the left was definitely his father. Ravi recognized him from his old photographs. He was possibly in his mid-twenties when the picture was taken. He was dressed in a kurta-pajama. The man to the right of the picture was also wearing a kurta-pajama. He seemed to be the same age as his father. However, he was shorter and a good bit heavier. He also had a moustache. It was the man standing between the two of them, however, who made Ravi catch his breath.

He was a stocky, light-skinned man of medium height in

his mid-thirties. He was cleanshaven, with short black hair, a snub nose and a wide mouth. He was wearing a kurta and a dhoti tied Marathi style with the folds largely collected over the right hip. He stood, smiling at the camera, with his arms thrown round the men standing to his right and left.

He was Nathuram Vinayak Godse – the man who assassinated Mahatma Gandhi.

Seven

"I am writing my Ph.D. thesis on the Hindu nationalist movement in the 1940's," Sapna said. "While doing my research I got this picture. It was given to me by Ajit Munje. He's the man on the right of the picture."

Ravi was still staring at the picture. His father and Nathuram Godse! *You don't really know me*, his father had said when he had called him from America after receiving his letter. Could he have meant this?

"This photograph was taken in Poona in 1947," Sapna continued. "What you see in the background is the office of the newspaper that Godse edited. It was a Marathi paper called *The Agrani*. That means the leader. *The Agrani* was a rabid Hindu nationalist paper – so rabid, in fact, it was shut down by the Bombay provincial government in 1947. Not for long, though. Barely ten days later it surfaced under a new name – *Hindu Rashtra* or the Hindu Nation.

"Yesterday when your father returned my call, I told him about this picture and Ajit Munje. He didn't say anything for a long time. I thought the phone had been disconnected. I was about to hang up when he finally spoke. He said he'd have to call me back."

So his father had gone to the public telephone booth to talk to her.

"He called about thirty minutes later," Sapna said. "He said I had taken him completely by surprise. He hadn't heard from Ajit Munje in over fifty years and had thought that he was dead. I told him he was very much alive and dearly wanted to see him. Your father said he was keen to meet him as well. But it had to wait until today, since you were coming from America last night. He said he'd call me today and set up a time. But then this morning I read about his death in the newspaper."

"What was Ajit Munje to my father?" Ravi asked.

"Your father lived with Ajit Munje and his family from 1944 to 1948."

"Where?"

"In Poona."

"That's impossible. My father was a refugee from Rawalpindi. He didn't set foot in, what we call India today, until after partition."

"That's what he may have told you. But he was very much in Poona in the 1940's, writing for Godse's newspaper."

"What?"

"That's the truth."

"I don't believe it. Okay, let's say he was in Poona. But that doesn't change the fact that my father was a Punjabi. And you yourself said Godse's newspaper was in Marathi. Even the very thought of him writing for a Marathi newspaper is laughable."

Ravi's voice was raised. The people, seated at the other tables, glanced in his direction. Sapna got up.

"Where are you going?" Ravi asked.

"I didn't come here to be told that I'm a liar," she said.

"I'm sorry."

He rose and placed his hand on her arm.

"Sapna, listen to me," he said. "This time yesterday I couldn't have been happier. I was on my way here to take my father back with me to America. After the death of my mother, there was nothing I wanted more.

"Yet now, rather than taking my father back with me, I'm going to cremate him. You probably have parents, brothers, sisters, cousins, aunts, uncles … All I had left was my father. And now I don't even have him. My father didn't die in an accident. He was murdered. And I need to know who did it. I don't know what you just told me has to do with it. But I am sure it fits in somehow. To know how, however, I need to know everything."

He gazed at her, his eyes practically beseeching her. She looked down. Then she took a deep breath and said, "Come with me."

She had come by bus. So they took his car. She directed the

chauffeur to take them to Munirka – a middle-class neighborhood close to Jawaharlal Nehru University. She lived there in an apartment with her grandfather. Her parents, she said, were dead.

Within ten minutes, they were outside her building. It was a gray-colored, four-story building – part of an apartment complex surrounded on all sides by a ten-foot high fence of corrugated iron. Sapna told the chauffeur he could park the car in the visitors' section. Then she invited Ravi up.

She lived on the third floor. Ravi followed her up a staircase that wound its way up on one side of the building. Soon they were outside her front door. She unlocked it, and they went in.

"Is that you, Sapna?" a man's voice called out.

Ravi entered the flat to find himself in the drawing room. A thickset old man, dressed in a white kurta-pajama, was seated on the sofa in front of the television, which was on.

"This is Ajit Munje," Sapna said. "My grandfather."

Eight

Munje was heavier than he looked in the picture. Over the years, his hair, too, had thinned and turned white. His moustache had a fair sprinkling of gray, and he was wearing glasses.

Sapna introduced Ravi. Still recovering from the shock of learning that Munje was her grandfather, Ravi started to fold his hands. The old man, however, clambered to his feet and hugged him in a tight embrace. When he finally released him, Ravi could see his eyes shining with tears. He was taken aback. He had never seen the old man before.

Sapna asked him to sit down. Ravi settled in one of the two overstuffed chairs placed diagonally to the right of the sofa. The chairs were separated by a small side table. A larger table, rectangular in shape, stood in the middle of the room. A red carpet covered the floor. The television set, which was still on, sat on a low table across the room from the sofa. The room was about half the size of the drawing room in Ravi's house in Vasant Vihar.

Sapna switched off the TV and sat down on the sofa next to her grandfather.

"You look just like your father," Munje said to Ravi. "Same eyes, same nose, same height ... When you came in, for a second I thought we were back in 1948 and your father had just walked into the room."

He sighed.

"I was so looking forward to seeing him again," he said. "I hadn't seen him in more than fifty years, since 1948. Then, just two days ago, I saw an article in *The Republic* about his retirement. It gave a rundown of his entire career of more than fifty years with the newspaper. There was a photograph there that had been taken during his youth. I recognized him immediately, even though the name he was using was different."

"What do you mean the name he was using was different?" Ravi asked.

"Ashish Malhotra."

"That was his name."

"No, his real name was Ranbir Lal."

Ravi stared at him.

"What the hell are you talking about?" he said. "My father's name was Ashish Malhotra."

Munje turned to Sapna.

"Sapna, go to my desk," he said. "There, right on top, you will find an old biography of Srinivas Ramanujam. Please bring it."

She left and soon returned with a thickly bound book.

"We were all avid readers in those days," Munje said. "Therefore, on birthdays, we invariably gave each other books. Your father gave me this in 1947 – one of the first biographies of Srinivas Ramanujam, that, too, by an Englishman. A man may change many things about himself, but not his handwriting."

He opened the book. Ravi rose from his chair and came over to the sofa. Munje pointed to the page he had opened. Putting on his glasses, Ravi leaned forward to get a better look. Then his eyes widened.

The page, in front of him, was blank, except for a note written with a blue pen. Over the years, the writing had dimmed somewhat. But it was still easily legible. It read:

To my dear friend Ajit with many happy returns of the day.

Ranbir

Poona, June 12, 1947

The words had been constructed in such a way that all the letters were erect. The T's were only half-crossed. The I's and the J in Ajit were missing the dot on top ... It was, without a doubt, the same handwriting Ravi had read in countless letters from his father.

He turned to Munje. He was struck speechless. He had thought himself incapable of being surprised any further that day. But this ...

Munje patted him on the shoulder and made him sit on the sofa. Ravi sat still, staring straight in front of him.

His father clearly hadn't been the person he had believed him to be. Then *who* had he been? And how did he become Ashish Malhotra?

Part Two

Nine

"I was at the Indian National Congress session in Nagpur in 1920. There Mahatma Gandhi promised freedom within the year. It is now 1937. Where is freedom?"

If there was one word to describe the speaker, it was thin – thin voice, thin hair, thin face, thin frame ... That day he wore a thin cotton kurta with his dhoti as well. And when he strove to be emphatic, as he did when making the point about freedom, he did so by wagging a thin forefinger at the audience.

Meet Sadashiv Gokhale – a forty-five-year-old widower, speaking in Delhi in his capacity as a pracharak or organizer for a young Hindu organization called the Rashtriya Swayamsevak Sangh or the RSS.

He was standing under a banyan tree. Behind him stood three young men, one of whom was his son, Aditya, dressed in the RSS uniform of khaki shorts, a white short-sleeved shirt and a black cap. The yellow-green foliage of the tree hung above them. It was so dense that even the thick banyan branches disappeared from sight. The July sun, however, still found a way to leak through it all, landing on the shaded ground in tiny drops, so that the entire area under the tree appeared to be a net made up of light and shade.

Some fifty young men were in attendance to Sadashiv Gokhale. Most of them were there out of curiosity. They had heard about this organization out of Nagpur that promised to organize the Hindus on the same paramilitary lines as the Muslim Khaksars. So they had come to hear this representative sent into their midst. A few, however, were already members, as their RSS uniforms attested. They were there as volunteers to hand out literature. And then there were a few like Ranbir Lal – a sixteen-year-old, from the nearby orphanage, who was there by invitation.

Sadashiv Gokhale continued.

"What will Mahatma Gandhi and his nonviolence do, except perpetuate the cowardice that so many years of slavery have made an integral part of the Hindu character? There are one hundred and fifty thousand people in Nagpur. Of these one hundred and thirty thousand are Hindu and only twenty thousand Muslim. Yes, only twenty thousand. Yet the Hindus are scared of the Muslims!

"But what can be more demeaning than the fact that today more than two hundred and fifty million Hindus are enslaved by 2,000 civil servants, 10,000 military officers and 60,000 soldiers – 72, 000 Britishers in all?

"Why is it that throughout history the Hindu nation has been unable to repel invaders? First the Turks and the Afghans, then the Mughals, and now the British. Why?

"It is because we Hindus are divided; we are divided by language, caste, creed ... We are so divided there are those who say we are not even a nation.

"Make no mistake about it. We Hindus are a nation. Our blood and culture are one and the land from the Indus River in the north to the Indian Ocean in the south is our motherland. We, in the RSS, want us Hindus to reclaim that motherland. But we cannot do that by perpetuating the scourge of cowardice as Gandhiji proposes. We have to root it out. We have to learn to fight, not turn the other cheek. Then only we will get our nation back. Then only we will have Hindutva."

He finished with the RSS salute – thumb pressed against the chest, with the palm down. Some in the crowd began to leave. Others approached Sadashiv Gokhale with questions. And still others went up to the RSS volunteers to ask for literature.

Aditya came over to Ranbir.

"Come, meet my father," he said.

Ten

Four months ago in March, when Ranbir first met Aditya, attending a speech by a Hindu nationalist like Sadashiv Gokhale wouldn't have entered his wildest dreams. Then politics, if anything, was the last thing on his mind. All his waking hours (and, for that matter, a good part of his dreaming) were taken up by his matriculation examination coming up in April.

In those days, ten grades were all you had in school. The matric exam, held at the end of the tenth year, was a make or break test. It was, in effect, a college entrance examination. How you did in it determined which college you entered, whether or not you got a scholarship, or, for that matter, whether you got to go to college at all. Even if you didn't want to go to college, you still had to pass the examination. To get just about any respectable job, you had to be at least matric pass.

For a poor orphan like Ranbir, consumed with the idea of going to college, it was imperative not simply to do well, but do well enough to get a scholarship. Otherwise, there was no way he was going to be able to pay for college.

Realizing that, Ranbir hit his books with everything he had. At all times of the day (and most of the night), he could be found with his nose buried in some textbook. He ate sparingly and slept even less. He had no time for friends or conversation. Not that he had too many friends, for that matter; at the best of times, he was a brooding loner with little to say to anyone. But even for him, in those final weeks before the matric exam, he retreated into a shell.

The cost, all those days and nights of cramming were exacting, was plain to see. His eyes were hemmed in by dark circles. His face, which was already angular, became even smaller as his cheeks sank. His wiry frame began to look skeletal, as whatever flesh it possessed started rolling off ... In fact, he shrank so much, there were those that worried that he might disappear.

Watching him, the other boys at the orphanage were befuddled, to say the least. The way they saw it, Ranbir was sure to pass the examination, which wasn't something many of them could say for themselves. As a matric pass, he'd have no problems landing a cushy office job as a clerk or maybe even an accountant. So why was he breaking his back to get that elusive scholarship? His future, as far as they were concerned, was assured, irrespective of whether he went to college or not.

But then it wasn't the first time they'd found Ranbir an enigma. Rather, it was something that happened quite regularly.

You see, Ranbir, quite simply, was different. He didn't look it. In fact, on the surface, he appeared rather ordinary. He was gangly to-the point of gawkiness, with a slight stoop in the shoulders. He dressed carelessly, often donning shirts stained with ink or food. When he spoke, which wasn't often, it was in a low hesitant voice . . . In fact, from all appearances, he seemed headed for a life of anonymity.

The maniac zeal with which he hit his books, however, provided the first whiff of the fire raging in his belly. The fact he had topped his class, year in year out, since the fourth grade was ample proof that the hunger, apparent in his face, was more than skin deep. That he lived in an orphanage filled with school dropouts made his academic accomplishments that much more creditable.

Ironically, these very same accomplishments also conspired with his quiet disposition to make him lonely. Many in the orphanage mistook his silence for aloofness brought about by his academic success. With the result, he had few friends. Little did anyone realize, however, that his solitary nature, far from being aloof, actually hid a dark melancholy side.

The fact that he was an orphan, who didn't even know who his parents had been, weighed heavily on Ranbir. The barbs, such a background invited at school, stung him sharply. Everyone knew he had been found abandoned on the doorstep of the orphanage when he was barely three months old. Even his name had come from the director of the orphanage. Not a week went by when someone did not remind him of those circumstances. An especially painful instance, from which he never fully recovered, occurred when he was eight. A classmate told the teacher, in front of the entire class, that his parents didn't want him sitting next to Ranbir, because he could very well be the bastard son of a prostitute. Ranbir cried himself to sleep for weeks after that day.

In fact, if he hadn't discovered his photographic memory and the natural ability he had with words, Ranbir might have dropped out of school like others at the orphanage. Academic success, however, helped blunt some of the pain. It silenced some of his worst detractors and garnered praise and favor from teachers. Most importantly, it held out the promise of a better future.

It was with an eye at that future that Ranbir threw himself into his preparation for his matriculation examination. As part of that preparation, one March morning, he rose early and bicycled the four miles to school to attend a math tutorial. By then, all tenth grade students were officially on preparatory leave. The math teacher, however, had said he'd drill anyone who showed up that morning. Ranbir was more than keen to take him up on the offer, as math was his weakest subject.

On reaching the school, he headed straight for the parking lot for bicycles – a dusty stretch of land surrounded by a wire fence. The breeze had picked up. With the result, dust was blowing all over the parking lot. After parking his bicycle,

Ranbir, who was dressed in a kurta-pajama and a pair of rubber slippers, was forced to walk, holding his pajama almost up to his knees in a bid to save it from the dust swarming all over his feet and ankles. He was so engrossed in that endeavor he failed to notice Aditya. With the result, he almost walked into him.

"Careful," Aditya said, steadying Ranbir.

Although he was a year younger than Ranbir, he stood almost a head taller. He was also much more powerfully built. Like Ranbir he was wearing a kurta-pajama. However, he didn't appear to mind the dust flying about.

He gave Ranbir a friendly grin and extended his hand.

"I am Aditya Gokhale," he said.

Another boy, parking his bicycle, shouted, "What are you doing with him? He doesn't even know the name of his parents. For all you know he could be the bastard son of a prostitute."

Ranbir swallowed. It was the same boy, who had told the teacher in front of the entire class that his parents didn't want him sitting next to Ranbir. Even now, eight years later, the memory hurt..

Aditya, however, descended on the boy.

"Who are you to say such things about him?" he demanded. "He doesn't know the name of his parents. Well, what are your parents? A peon in the police commissioner's office, a cook at his residence – a couple of lapdogs of the British. What do you know his parents might have been freedom fighters who died for the country?"

Ranbir's eyes opened wide, as the other boy dropped his head and walked away.

O, to see one of his detractors slink away as he himself had from him on so many occasions; Ranbir enjoyed that. In a matter of minutes, Aditya had accomplished something Ranbir could only fantasize about for eight years. He turned to Aditya, with eyes bright with admiration, already exuding the deference of a follower in the presence of a leader.

That moment set the tone for their relationship. Although Aditya was younger than Ranbir and new to the school, it was Ranbir who looked up to Aditya. It wasn't hard to see why. Unlike Ranbir, Aditya was assertive. If the situation warranted, he was more than happy to get into a scrap. A trained wrestler, he usually had the last word in a fight. With the result, no one messed with him. Ranbir came to be seen as a friend of Aditya. Consequently, the other kids stopped picking on him as well. Needless to say, he found that gratifying.

Even more than that, however, Aditya offered Ranbir something of which he had been starved his entire life. Unlike everyone he had met so far, Aditya didn't seem to care about his antecedents. He treated him as a person. For Ranbir that was exhilarating, to say the least.

Later, when he became part of the RSS, Ranbir realized what Aditya was doing was standard practice. RSS activists consciously reached out to people living on the fringes of Hindu society, such as orphans. They believed, over there, they had a ready pool of potential recruits who'd be attracted by the camaraderie that comes with being part of a group. Furthermore, bringing such people into the fold was consistent with the RSS goal of creating a united Hindu society.

In his conversations with Ranbir, Aditya spent a lot of time talking about the RSS. He handed Ranbir RSS literature and invited him to come hear his father speak. Ranbir heard him out and politely thumbed through the literature. But he failed to show any real interest in the RSS.

Quite simply, he had other things on his mind. First, it was the matriculation examination. Once that was over, the interminable wait of three months for the results began. As the date in question crept closer, Ranbir found it hard to eat or sleep. On the night before, he was beside himself with anticipation. He showed up in school well before the results were posted on the notice board and spent anxious hours pacing. When the peon finally arrived with the result sheets, it was all Ranbir could do to stop himself from snatching them out of his hands.

Swallowing, he scanned the list for his roll number. When he finally located it, he couldn't believe what he saw. He remained where he was standing. Impatient students jostled him from all sides. But he didn't appear to notice them, as he stood rooted to the spot.

When he finally turned to make his way out of the crowd of students, he was staggering rather than walking. He looked as if he had just been dealt a mighty blow. His jaw was slack, his eyes glazed and his face drained of blood.

He went out into the playing field and collapsed on to a wooden bench to sit still, staring fixedly into the distance.

He had stood first in the entire district. But the scholarship had gone to someone else.

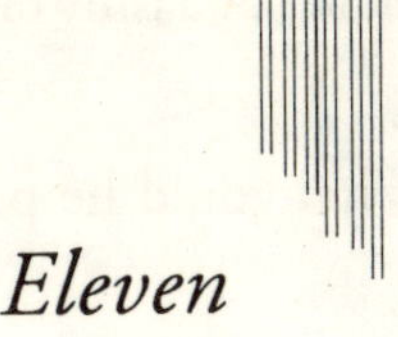

Eleven

After finishing his speech, Sadashiv Gokhale spent a few minutes talking to the members of the audience who had come up to him. Then he had a word with the RSS volunteers who had been distributing literature. Finally, he dismissed the volunteers and sat down, crosslegged, under the banyan tree. Ranbir and Aditya settled on the grass in front of him.

"My son told me about you," he said to Ranbir. "In the matric exam you stood first in the entire district. Yet the scholarship went to a boy who got lesser marks – a Muslim boy."

Ranbir nodded.

"Why was that?" Sadashiv Gokhale asked.

"It is government policy to get adequate communal representation in the colleges," Ranbir said. "So they chose to give the scholarship to someone from a minority community."

"Do you think that's fair?"

Ranbir stared at the ground.

"No," he said.

"Then what are you going to do about it?" Sadashiv Gokhale demanded.

Ranbir didn't know what to say. What could he possibly do?

"The worst thing you can do is do nothing," Sadashiv Gokhale continued. "That's why we Hindus are in the sorry state that we are today. Because we have got used to doing nothing."

He paused briefly. Then he said, "Today we have the British ruling India. Do you think things will be any different tomorrow if we have Gandhi and the Indian National Congress? Then, will Hindu boys like you see their dreams come true?"

Again he paused and gazed at Ranbir who was looking nonplussed.

"When a Muslim so much as squeals Gandhi goes on a hunger strike," Sadashiv Gokhale said. "Yet when the Muslim Khaksars go out and terrorize Hindus he doesn't lift a finger. What do you think will happen if the party he dominates comes to power? Do you think for a moment that they will stand up for the Hindus?"

He leaned forward, his eyes boring into Ranbir.

"Make no mistake about it," he said. "Sooner or later the British will be forced to leave India. Then we Hindus will have to fight the Muslims for our rightful place in this country.

We have to get ready for that day. Already Gandhi has pushed us back several years with his policy of nonviolence. So there is not a moment to lose. Nothing less than the survival of the Hindu nation is hanging in the balance, and it is the duty of every Hindu to heed the call."

With those words, he rose to his feet. He was due to speak somewhere else and he was already running late. Aditya and he took leave. Ranbir went back home, with Sadashiv Gokhale's words ringing in his ears.

For the rest of the day, he could think of little else. By the time he went to bed that night, he had come to a decision. He was going to join the RSS.

The next day Ranbir joined the RSS. Given the fact his orphanage depended on the philanthropy of Parsi industrialists sympathetic to the Indian National Congress, he did join incognito. His uniform remained hidden at the local RSS branch office and he only wore it at sunrise to the daily ritual of prayers, lessons and exercises. Furthermore, he made sure that no RSS literature ever found its way into the orphanage. In addition, if any of his RSS comrades ever visited him there, they did so incognito.

He was not unique at the time. The British, apprehensive of the paramilitary nature of the RSS, worked hard to stunt its growth. In some areas, teachers in government schools were barred from joining. In others, the ban was extended to all local government employees. With the result, there were plenty of incognito members in the 1930's.

Exactly where did Ranbir fit into the RSS? Well, certainly not in its kshatriya or warrior world view. In fact, he wasn't even a speck on that horizon.

Two mornings was all it took for him to accumulate enough aches and pains to cry off morning drill. And lathi instruction? God, to swing that five-foot bamboo stick about ... Ranbir tried his hand at it and promptly gave up after knocking himself on the head. And gym work? Barbells, iron-topped maces with wooden handles, wrestling bouts ... Suffice to say, Ranbir was no poster boy for the muscular Hindu. That distinction belonged to men like Aditya.

No, very early on in his career as an RSS volunteer, he gravitated towards the press.

Sadashiv Gokhale had established a weekly newspaper in Hindi called *The Arya*. The word arya, of course, is derived from aryan. Given the fact that Delhi is in north India and most north Indians claim aryan origin, the choice of the name was astute.

The Arya was not officially an RSS newspaper. The first Sarsanghchalak or Supreme Leader of the RSS, Dr. Keshav Hedgewar, thought publicity would commercialize the RSS and compromise its function of character building. With the result, the RSS published no journals or newspapers until well after Hedgewar's death.

However, within the RSS, there was a group that considered Hedgewar far too passive and esoteric. That group wanted the RSS to push its agenda aggressively and become a major player in national and local politics.

Sadashiv Gokhale belonged to that group. He had long been an admirer of Veer Savarkar. He dearly wanted to infuse some Savarkarlike activism into the RSS.

By 1937 Vinayak Damodar Savarkar, better known as Veer 'The Brave' Savarkar, had emerged as the pre-eminent figure in the Hindu nationalist movement. Elected president of the leading Hindu organization of the day – the Hindu Mahasabha or the Great Hindu Assembly – Savarkar was also the author of *Hindutva* – the book that had become the Hindu nationalist bible. His reputation, however, extended well beyond Hindu nationalist circles. He had caught the nation's imagination in 1910 by jumping into the sea near Marseilles to escape British custody. He was then being shipped to India, after being arrested for his anti-British activities as an Indian student in Britain. His recapture and subsequent incarceration in the dreaded jail in the Andaman and Nicobar Islands only added to his popularity. When he was finally released under public pressure in 1924, he emerged from jail a bonafide hero, admired even by moderate Hindus. For men like Sadashiv Gokhale, he was a demigod.

The Arya was backed financially by two Delhi businessmen who were, like Sadashiv Gokhale, Savarkarites. Everyone who wrote for it belonged either to the Hindu Mahasabha or the militant wing of the RSS. Given Dr. Hedgewar's views on publicity, all the RSS people wrote under pseudonyms. (Ranbir's, rather interestingly, was Naveen Paranjpye, which would make him Marathi.) And while Sadashiv Gokhale called the shots, the official proprietors listed were the two Delhi businessmen.

Ranbir wrote extensively for *The Arya*. Stories, opinions, editorials ... he did it all. Since seniority was so big in the RSS scheme of things, the fact he was allowed to write at all, while being a teenager, was in itself an anomaly. That he was close to Aditya and, therefore by extension, Sadashiv Gokhale certainly helped his cause. But more than anything, the explanation lay in the fact that *The Arya* was something of an undercover operation. In order to keep the secret, Sadashiv Gokhale needed a staff he could trust. And who could he trust more than Ranbir – a boy who had been raised a Punjabi and yet was so enamored with him and his son that not only had he adopted a Marathi pseudonym, he was also taking the trouble to learn Marathi, the Gokhales' native language?

As far as the content of his writing went, Ranbir stayed true to the standard *Arya* line. He called for Hindu unity and lamented Hindu cowardice, urging the community to shed it by adopting the warrior lifestyle propagated by the RSS. He extolled Hindu revivalist heroes, such as Chhattrapati Shivaji, Swami Vivekananda and Veer Savarkar, and denounced the people the movement saw as its enemies – the Muslims, the British and the Indian National Congress.

The work he did for *The Arya* afforded him a small income. He supplemented that by working as a clerk for a pickle manufacturer sympathetic to Hindu nationalism. This was a job he got at the recommendation of Sadashiv Gokhale. By the time he was eighteen, he had saved enough money to move out of the orphanage and get his own room in old Delhi.

Thus it was he entered 1940.

Twelve

On June 21, 1940, Dr. Hedgewar died in Nagpur. Aditya and Sadashiv Gokhale prepared to travel there to pay their final respects.

"We won't be away for long," Aditya assured Ranbir. "Hedgewar Guruji would have picked a successor. Soon we will know who he is. And once he takes charge my father and I should be on our way back to Delhi."

"But who will he be?" Ranbir asked him.

"I want it to be Savarkar Guruji. That will unite the RSS and the Mahasabha. But from what my father has heard, it is going to be Appaji Joshi. He is the seniormost RSS leader. Anyway, whoever it is, we will know soon and then my father and I will be on our way back."

As it turned out, it was four years before Ranbir saw him again.

In the next four years, Ranbir not only quit the RSS, he practically quit the path of Hindu nationalism.

After joining the RSS, he had enjoyed the patronage of Sadashiv Gokhale. However, once it became clear that the

Gokhales were not returning to Delhi, he was as exposed as any volunteer in his local RSS branch; in fact, more so, because he had once been privileged. For Sadashiv Gokhale's successor sought to create his own cadre of loyalists, viewing anyone who had been close to his predecessor with a good deal of suspicion. Consequently, Ranbir found himself being marginalized. For some time, his involvement in *The Arya* brought a measure of satisfaction. But the lack of interest in the paper shown by Sadashiv Gokhale's successor, coupled with souring relations between Hedgewar's successor and Veer Savarkar, queered the situation. As the paper was funded by a couple of Savarkarites, the individuals connected with the RSS found themselves being eased out. Ranbir, too, could not escape the axe.

Increasingly depressed with life, Ranbir withdrew not just from the RSS but, for all intents and purposes, from Hindu nationalism. This withdrawal was particularly telling, as it provided a glimpse as to how committed he was to the Cause in the first place.

Let's compare his commitment to that of Aditya.

For Aditya, Hindu nationalism was the prism through which he saw life, the guideline he applied to interpret its intricacies, the rulebook that governed his actions . . . He was someone who could disagree with tactics, but never the Cause. With the result, he could part ways with Hindu nationalists, but never the path of Hindu nationalism.

Ranbir's commitment, however, lacked such a firm foundation. His membership in the RSS accrued as a consequence of his resentment over losing his scholarship. The favor he received after joining, thanks to his closeness to the Gokhales, cheered him up no end. However, did Hindu nationalism ever become an end in itself for him? Not really. For, unlike Aditya, the prism through which Ranbir saw life changed constantly, its makeup determined by the moment more than anything else. Therefore, the view he was likely to get after losing favor was bound to be very different from the one he had when the Gokhales were in town. With the result, not surprisingly after the Gokhales left, he experienced the same sense of letdown he'd had when he lost his scholarship.

Then why, in 1944, did he leave Delhi for Poona to join a Hindu nationalist outfit?

Because his only friend Aditya was in it. Furthermore, given his situation at the time, it wasn't as if he had any other option.

He had lost his position at *The Arya*. He had been sidelined to the point of quitting his local RSS branch. Then, in 1943, he got the pink slip at his clerical job as well, as the pickle manufacturer, he was working for, was forced to cut back in the recession caused by the Second World War. With few jobs to be had and no one like Sadashiv Gokhale around to put in a word for him, he was forced to scrounge, doing a series of menial jobs merely to stay afloat. Practically homeless and never knowing where his next meal was coming from, he was miserable.

That was when he received a letter from Aditya, asking him to come to Poona.

Thirteen

Yes, Poona not Nagpur. A lot had changed in Aditya's life as well, since he and his father left Delhi for Nagpur to pay their final respects to Dr. Hedgewar.

Twelve days after Dr. Hedgewar's death, on July 3rd, 1940, his successor was announced. To say Aditya was surprised by the choice would be an understatement. The same day he wrote to Ranbir:

I am in shock. It is not Savarkar Guruji or even Joshiji. It is Madhav Sadashiv Golwalkar. What possessed Hedgewar Guruji to pick a man like Golwalkar to be our Sarsanghchalak I can't imagine? Golwalkar was only recently promoted to the highest levels of the RSS. He has no experience whatsoever of politics. In fact, in 1936, he actually abandoned everything he was doing and, without a word to anyone, went to live with Swami Akhandanand in Bengal. He only returned after Swami Akhandanand died in 1937. What can such a man do for the RSS? Really, the last thing we need is a fakir at our helm …

The choice of Golwalkar put paid to any plans Aditya and his father had of a swift return to Delhi. It caused a lot of consternation in the RSS ranks, leaving many senior officials like Sadashiv Gokhale uncertain of their future. For Golwalkar was something of an unknown quantity, and no one was quite sure of what he was going to do.

Well, one of the first things he did do was move to consolidate his authority. A pracharak or organizer, who reported directly to Golwalkar rather than the sanghchalak or the provincial leader, was appointed for each province. The intent was clear. Golwalkar wanted to create a cadre of officials loyal to him.

The appointment of such organizers effectively killed any chance of Aditya and his father going back to Delhi. On August 12, 1940, Aditya wrote to Ranbir:

I am sorry to inform you that we will not be coming back to Delhi.

It has taken my father a long time to make up his mind, and it has been a painful decision. But in the present circumstances, I don't think he has a choice.

Now each province is going to have a pracharak who reports directly to Mr. Golwalkar. It is clear this position is designed to undercut the provincial officials by installing someone who can report on them. In such a scenario, it is impossible for my father to continue with his duties in Delhi ...

Aditya remained less than impressed with Golwalkar for the rest of 1940. Unlike similar-minded volunteers, however, he did not quit the RSS; his father's roots in the organization went far too deep. However, he noted its changing nature with increasing dissatisfaction. In particular, he found Golwalkar's refusal to involve the RSS in political activity maddening.

Then, in early 1941, Aditya met Veer Savarkar for the first time. On January 20, he described the meeting in his letter to Ranbir:

Last week I had the honor of visiting Savarkar Sadan with some of our brothers. You wouldn't believe the number of people that go there for Savarkar Guruji's blessings every day. Because there are so many, usually you have to wait for hours. But one of our brothers, Nathuram Godse, was well known to Guruji. So we were ushered into his presence without any delay.

The minute you look into Guruji's eyes, you know you are in the presence of a great man. When he talks, you cannot help but listen. We are truly lucky to have someone like him to look out for our community.

He took a moment to talk to each one of us personally. It is a moment I will treasure for the rest of my life. I was so nervous I could not get a word out. He was amused. He patted me on the shoulder and told me to keep up the good work ...

A few months after he met Savarkar, Aditya lost his father due to a heart attack. Since the appointment of Golwalkar, the elder Gokhale had increasingly found himself marginalized in the highest echelons of the RSS. It was no secret that

Golwalkar and Savarkar did not see eye to eye. Therefore, Sadashiv Gokhale's open admiration for Savarkar was sure to place him on Golwalkar's wrong side. Then Sadashiv Gokhale did himself no favors by suggesting, in one of his earliest meetings with Golwalkar, that the RSS merge with the Mahasabha.

The death of his father only served to increase Aditya's discontent with Golwalkar. With mounting disquiet, he watched Golwalkar undo the work people like his father had done in building relations with the Mahasabha and move the RSS closer to the Indian National Congress. When he learned that Congress leaders were going to preside over RSS functions, he was outraged. His sense of outrage only deepened when he got to know that Golwalkar had not only refused to raise new paramilitary units, he was also opposing the Mahasabha's drive to enlist Hindus in the military. He wrote to Ranbir:

Has Mr. Golwalkar lost his mind? Anyone with an iota of common sense can see the British are not going to be able to hold on to India after the war. Then we will have to fight the Muslims for our rightful place in India. Therefore, it is imperative we use the war years to get ready ...

The break, however, came when Golwalkar terminated the military department of the RSS on April 29, 1943. The next day, Aditya quit the RSS and made his way to Poona to join a new Hindu militant outfit – one that had Savarkar's blessing.

It was called the Hindu Rashtra Dal or the Hindu National Force.

A little more than eight months later, he wrote his final letter to Ranbir:

We are going to start a paper at the request of Savarkar Guruji. When I heard about it, I immediately met Nathuram Godse, who is going to be its editor, and Narayan Apte, who will be its business manager, and told them about the work you did for The Arya. *They were impressed. They were even more impressed by the fact that, despite being a Punjabi, you picked up Marathi and can write, as well as speak it well. For proof I showed them your letters to me, which are all in Marathi. The paper, incidentally, will also be in Marathi.*

They want you to come here as soon as possible. I am hoping you will. I have been waiting for years for the day when, once again, we will be together and working side by side to realize the dream we share. Please come.

Fourteen

When Ranbir arrived in Poona, Aditya put him up with another member of the Dal – a schoolteacher named Ajit Munje. As he explained to Ranbir, the room he was living in was simply too small for two people. Munje, on the other hand, had a house. Therefore, Ranbir would be much better off with him and his family. Ranbir protested initially. The last thing he wanted to do in a new city was live with strangers. When he saw Aditya's room, however, he had to admit that Aditya was right.

Ajit Munje was a couple of years older than Ranbir. A married man, with a six-month-old daughter, he was originally from Ahmednagar – a city 60 miles from Poona. Coming from a devout Hindu family, he was a teacher of mathematics. While still in Ahmednagar, he had met Godse's right-hand man, Narayan Apte. At the time, Apte was teaching at a local American mission high school. Although Apte was almost ten years older than Munje, the two became fast friends. Other than a staunchly Hindu background, they also shared a common subject; they both taught mathematics.

In 1943 Munje approached Apte, who was now in Poona,

with a plea for help. Munje had gotten married the year before. Now a baby was on the way. On what he was making in his current job, he could barely make ends meet for himself and his wife. He didn't know what he was going to do once the baby came along. He begged Apte to help him find a job that paid better. He was willing to relocate to Poona, if necessary.

Apte got him a job teaching at a private school in Poona. Munje moved to Poona with his wife. At Apte's behest, he joined the Hindu Rashtra Dal. He had never been interested in politics. But Apte was keen for him to be a part of the Dal and Munje, already beholden to Apte, felt he owed him at least that much.

Joining the Dal, however, did nothing to change Munje's mindset towards politics. He attended a couple of meetings and showed up for the odd political rally. But more often than not, he had a ready excuse to be absent. When it came to making posters or posting fliers, he was even less forthcoming. He never volunteered for the job (in fact, he never volunteered for anything at the Dal), and, when it was forced upon him, had the notorious habit of missing deadlines.

The plain truth was that Ajit Munje was simply not cut out to be a political activist. He was far too easygoing, far too involved with his wife and daughter, far too immersed in day-to-day events ... He loved the good things of life. Whenever he had a few rupees, he could be found in a sweetshop, stuffing himself with laddoos. He was loath to spend a moment away from his wife and daughter. His idea of a good day included lots of sleep, food and time alone with his family. The grind of political activity was anathema to him.

It was this lack of involvement in the affairs of the Dal that stuck Munje with Ranbir. One day, Apte visited him with Aditya to ask him to host Aditya's friend who was coming all the way from Delhi. Apte told him such a gesture would convince everyone he was still a useful part of the Dal. The import of the message was clear. Munje hadn't been doing his bit; so now he had to do this to show that he was still willing to contribute.

Munje sighed. He wasn't too excited at the prospect of a stranger living in his house. But he couldn't afford to say no to Apte. He was still new to Poona and Apte knew a lot of people there. Then he owed Apte his job.

Reluctantly, he agreed to put up Ranbir.

The newspaper, Aditya had written Ranbir about, was *The Agrani*, which later became the *Hindu Rashtra*.

The men, behind *The Agrani* or the *Hindu Rashtra*, were not merely devout Hindus, they were also devoutly Marathi. Many of them had been members of the RSS. Some, like their leader Nathuram Godse, actually started out as followers of Mahatma Gandhi. Now, however, irrespective of past affiliation, they were united in their passion for Hindu nationalism.

How did Ranbir ease into their world?

Well, he actually managed quite well.

Agreed, because of his friendship with Aditya, he was welcome. However, he worked hard to imbed himself in the machinery of the Dal, seeking to compensate for the fact he was Punjabi as one might seek to encircle a fault.

Listen to Ranbir speak Marathi and you had to listen carefully to catch any trace of a Punjabi accent; all those hours, spent on his own in his room, dragging his voice through hour after hour of pronunciation. The real revelation, however, was his written Marathi. Most people remain locked in a paucity of confidence even after years of writing a foreign language. With the result, their writing never ventures off the beaten track. By the middle of 1945, however, Ranbir was displaying a supreme confidence in his articles and essays. On reading them, you were immediately struck by the suppleness of the sentences, the innovative combinations of words, the originality of the similes and metaphors . . . Not surprisingly, he began writing regularly for the newspaper in 1945. In a year and a half, he had honed his written Marathi sufficiently to go from gofer to leading contributor.

He wrote under his old pseudonym – Naveen Paranjpye. It made sense to have a Marathi name in a Marathi newspaper. In terms of content, he was decidedly strident. One article, he wrote on the Indian National Congress, was entitled “The Rapists of the Motherland,” another on Veer Savarkar “The

Avatar, the Messiah, the King," ... Needless to say, in the circles in which he was moving, the more extreme he was the more applause he received.

In addition, he worked hard to endear himself to Ajit Munje and his family. If Munje had been hesitant to take him in, his wife was even less pleased with the whole arrangement. With a baby in the house, the last thing she wanted was one more person to cook for and clean after. Furthermore, Ranbir was young and single. Young single men were known to be rambunctious and disruptive. They stayed out till all hours of the night, drank in excess, chased women ... What kind of impact would all that have on the baby? she demanded from her husband. Her husband told her that Ranbir was not that kind of man. He wouldn't be friends with Aditya if he were. However, he spoke without much conviction. The truth was that he himself was a bit apprehensive about having a young man living under the same roof as his wife.

On reaching Poona, Ranbir sized up the situation quickly and acted accordingly. Within days, he put any doubts, Munje may have had on his account, to rest by getting his wife to tie a rakhi on his wrist. That meant he considered her his sister. Furthermore, he indicated his willingness to pull his own weight in the house by helping out with the cooking and cleaning. In a matter of weeks, he transformed himself from an unwanted houseguest to a valued member of the household; so much sc that, six months later when he mentioned moving out, Munjc and his wife went to great pains to convince him to stay.

The way he set about making a place for himself in Poona was at sharp odds with everything he had done thus far in his life. Thus far he had allowed the fact that he was an orphan, and therefore an outsider, weigh him down like a disabled man may his disability. In Poona, however, he moved beyond that. Instead of letting what could be perceived as his disability get to him, he accepted it as a given and, instead, concentrated on finding ways to get what he wanted, in spite of it. This fundamental shift in attitude was not only key for him in Poona but, in subsequent years, in Delhi as well.

By the time India gained independence from Britain on August 15, 1947, Ranbir was well established in Poona. He had a home with Ajit Munje and his family. Thanks to his articles and essays, he had built up a small following in local Hindu nationalist circles. And though there wasn't much money in the newspaper, he knew enough people to get a steady supply of part-time jobs that allowed him to meet his day-to-day expenses. On the face of things, he should have been content. However, he was anything but …

Rather, he was wondering if the place he had made for himself was the one he wanted to occupy for the rest of his life. Life as an activist was spartan, at best. There was rarely any money for anything other than bare necessities. Even cigarettes were a luxury. (He had begun to smoke as an escape during his destitute days in Delhi.) Most of the time, he was forced to puff on the cheaper beedis. For someone like Aditya, who lived and died for the Cause, such an existence might be good enough. For Ranbir, however, it certainly wasn't.

Then matters at the Dal were taking a turn that made him decidedly nervous. It was one thing to write explosive articles in the newspaper. But now the talk was turning towards assassination and launching suicide attacks. The last thing Ranbir wanted was to be a martyr.

However, despite his growing discontent, he continued with his daily life, not giving anyone a hint of what was churning inside. With nothing else on the horizon, he was understandably hesitant to jeopardize what he had.

In January of 1948, however, the decision was taken out of his hands.

Fifteen

For India freedom had meant partition. The country was divided into two, with the Muslim-majority areas forming the nation of Pakistan and the Hindu-majority areas staying in India. It was believed the Hindu and Sikh minorities in Pakistan and the Muslim minority in India would continue to live in amity with the majority communities, as they had for centuries. That, however, did not happen. In Pakistan, Muslim gangs took to the streets, seeking to "cleanse" the area of Hindus and Sikhs, while Hindu and Sikh gangs retaliated in kind in India. The nerve center of the slaughter was Punjab, which had been split right down the middle at the time of partition. In both Punjabs, refugees crossed over to the other side in unprecedented numbers, multiplying, what was already an unparalleled human tragedy, several times.

By January of 1948, this pathetic drama had been played out for six months. Yet few could have visualized that its climax would be determined in a whitewashed shed in Poona that acted as the office of an obscure Hindu nationalist newspaper, which was now called the *Hindu Rashtra*.

It was early afternoon on January 13, 1948. Ranbir stood in front of the teleprinter in the office of the *Hindu Rashtra*. The teleprinter was spluttering out the same piece of news again and again. Ranbir stared at the repetitions drifting over his fingers to drop into a packing case filled with rolls of paper. Then he shouted, "Come and take a look at this," to the two other men in the shed – Nathuram Godse and Narayan Apte.

They came over. Ranbir stepped aside so that they could read the news off the teleprinter.

"Gandhi has begun a fast unto death," Apte read aloud.

He scanned the list of the Mahatma's demands, then turned to Godse, pointing to one of them. He didn't need to, as Godse's eyes were there already.

Gandhi wanted the Indian government to release the 550 million rupees Pakistan was supposed to receive as part of the independence settlement.

"We must stop him," Godse said. "This man has lost all touch with reality. The motherland has been chopped up. And he wants to reward the very same traitors that did it. While Hindu men are killed in the thousands in the streets and Hindu women jump into wells to save their honor, this man wants to help the very people responsible for these crimes; a bunch of murderers and rapists. We can't let that happen. Everything else we are doing must take a backseat. We can have only one aim now. We must kill Gandhi."

Apte agreed. The two men decided to meet in that office

that night to discuss how they would do it. Then they turned to Ranbir, who nodded quickly to indicate he'd be there as well. Godse and Apte left the shed, leaving Ranbir staring after them.

With shaking hands, Ranbir placed the khaki-colored beedi in his mouth. The first time he tried to light it, he dropped the match. Cursing, he took another match out of the matchbox. This time he was successful. Throwing away the match, he sucked on the beedi. It was a few drags before he was sufficiently calm.

Was Godse serious? Were they really going to do it?

In the past, several fanciful schemes, such as starting a guerilla campaign against the Nizam of Hyderabad and assassinating Mohammad Ali Jinnah, had been discussed. These discussions, rather than yielding any concrete plan of action, had degenerated into ranting and raving with no clear sense of purpose. With the result, they had never amounted to anything. This time, however, Ranbir had a hunch that things might be different. There had been something about the way Godse had spoken after reading the news off the teleprinter. His voice had been calm, his manner controlled. When he had walked out of the shed with Apte, his stride was sure … Quite frankly, he had scared the hell out of Ranbir.

Ranbir spent the next several hours on his own. He could feel that he had arrived at a crossroads and the moment was approaching when he had to make a choice. He wished he could speak to Aditya. But that was out of the question. Aditya had been gone since August. He was in Punjab, organizing Hindu militia groups against the Muslims, standing guard outside Hindu neighborhoods, setting up Hindu defense committees ... He considered talking to Ajit Munje and rejected the idea outright. Munje existed on the fringes of the Dal. Even if Godse and Apte were serious about making an attempt on Gandhi's life, it was unlikely that they'd involve Munje in the conspiracy. Moreover, given the fact that Munje was a man with a family, the less he knew about such things the better.

When night came, Ranbir headed for the office of the *Hindu Rashtra*. Instead of going in, however, he took up position behind a tree on the other side of the road. He saw four men, led by Godse, enter the shed. When they re-emerged, about an hour later, he was still standing outside. Taking care to stay out of sight, he followed them through Poona's streets. They went to the house of a man, who ran a bookstore and looked every inch a sadhu with his orange sarong, his long unkempt hair and his thick beard extending almost to his chest.

But Ranbir knew the man was no sadhu. The bookstore he ran was actually a front for his real trade that he practiced in a room at the back of the store; a room that contained all kinds of bombs, firearms, knives ...

The sadhu was really an arms peddler.

They were going to do it. Otherwise, they would never go to the arms peddler after their meeting.

Ranbir dug into his pockets for a beedi. All he found was the paper wrapping. He had smoked his last beedi earlier that night. With a curse, he threw away the wrapping.

Despite the fact it was a cool winter night, he was sweating. He dabbed his forehead with his handkerchief and swallowed.

There was no way he could go along with Godse and the others. He hadn't joined the Dal to be an assassin. Furthermore, even if they were able to get anywhere near Gandhi, it was unlikely they would emerge unscathed. Death or, at the very least, a long prison term was a certainty.

He glanced at his watch. The four men had been with the arms peddler for a half-hour now. They could be coming out any minute. When they did, there was a good chance they would go to Ajit Munje's house to find out why Ranbir hadn't made the meeting. So he had to act quickly.

He couldn't stay in Poona. If he did, he would have to go along with Godse and the others. There was no way he could opt out of the conspiracy, without paying with his life. Godse and company simply wouldn't run the risk of him going to the police behind their back. And given their network of friends and sympathizers, which included a number of policemen, they could hunt him down anywhere in Poona.

Without wasting another moment, he made his way to the railway station and caught the first train that wasn't going to Bombay. He knew Godse well enough to know that was where Godse would be going; Godse would never undertake such a momentous task as assassinating Gandhi before seeking the blessings of his guru Veer Savarkar.

The train he caught was bound for Ahmedabad. That, however, was not Ranbir's final destination. It is clear he selected that after some deliberation. For, at first thought, it seems like the last place where he should have wanted to go, since it was also the place where Godse and the others would be headed, once they were done with their guru.

Delhi.

But think about it for a minute. Even though Ranbir had been speaking Marathi for some time now, there were still occasions where he betrayed the fact he was Punjabi. Sometimes it was the way he pronounced a certain word, other times how he paused between sentences … There were times, too, when his accent slipped completely. It didn't happen often, and when it did he corrected it almost immediately. But still, while he might be able to write as Naveen Paranjpye, even now there were times when he found it hard to convince people that he had been born Naveen Paranjpye.

If he could be identified as an outsider in a state where he spoke the language fluently, he was bound to stick out even more in parts of India where he did not speak the language. And the last thing he wanted was to stick out; he was looking to get lost.

With the result, it was only natural for him to go to Delhi. Outside Punjab, which was going up in flames, the largest Punjabi population lived in Delhi. Furthermore, Delhi was his hometown – a city he knew better than any other – and, therefore, one where he could navigate a life away from what he was running far better than in a city that was foreign to him.

But more than all that, Delhi in 1948 was a city bursting with runaways. They came by the hundreds, then the thousands, then the hundreds of thousands ... There seemed no end to the amount the partitioned country appeared intent on ramming down the city's throat. They came from all over west Pakistan – from Sindh, Baluchistan, the Northwest Frontier Province ... But, most of all, they came from Punjab – from Lahore, Rawalpindi, Gujranwalla, Sialkot, Lyallpur ... In an unrelenting flood they overran the city's hotels, hovels, alleys, refugee camps, temples, pavements, and its Muslim neighborhoods. Yes, there were people running away from Delhi, as well. Given the amounts the city had to gulp, there were times it simply had to throw up.

So what was Ranbir? Just another runaway, just another Punjabi, just another arrival looking for a new beginning ... Yes, all in all, Delhi was a perfect place for him to get lost.

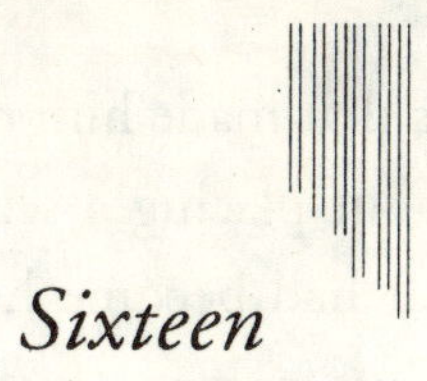

Sixteen

On his first day in Delhi, Ranbir found more people that wanted Gandhi dead than all his four years in Poona. He watched demonstrators make their way to Birla House, where the aged leader lay fasting, chanting, "Let Gandhi die." In the bustling alleys of the old city, in the brightly decorated arcades of Connaught Place and, most of all, in the refugee camps overflowing with people, filth and misery, he overheard innumerable conversations that hinged on one theme: When will that old man leave us alone? Yes, Delhi on January 15, 1948, was a city fed up of the Mahatma, as a child might be of a demanding father.

Yet the very next day, he gaped at Hindus, Muslims and Sikhs who had taken to the streets not to fight pitched battles, but link arms in peace brigades seeking signatures for petitions begging Gandhi to give up his fast. He stared at entire bazaars closed in solidarity with the Mahatma. He found himself surrounded by people asking each other: How can we save Gandhiji? ... Yes, as Gandhi's condition had worsened the city had somersaulted, as a child wishing to be rid of its father may when actually faced with the prospect.

In the ensuing days, he'd find alleys that made him retch, across which he could not walk without placing a scented handkerchief over his nose; alleys that had become horror museums, claiming as artifacts not just corpses, but also chopped fingers, toes and penises. Then there were alleys that nobody crossed; that were dark shrunken corridors hemmed in by squat brick houses. Once home to thousands of Muslims, they were now sites of flushing out operations being carried out by Hindu and Sikh gangs that entered them, shouting, "*Allah-o-Akbar*," only to hack to death any unsuspecting person who answered their call.

Most chilling of all, however, was the sight that greeted him when he stepped off the train at the Delhi railway station. There were four Sikhs, their blue turbans indicating they were Akalis, seated crosslegged on the cement platform in knee-length chogas. Each one of them was quiet, almost reverential, as he sat there with his eyes closed. All four of them could have been at a gurudwara on a Sunday, listening to a hymn or a granthi's sermon. Laid across each one's knees, however, was a naked kirpan, in one case with the curved blade edged with blood.

A friend, he made in Delhi, told him the Sikhs were refugees from Lahore. They were at the station to intercept any Muslims fleeing to Pakistan.

Waiting to intercept Muslims in January of 1948, when the deluge of migration caused by the partition of India had waned considerably … Still the Sikhs were at the station day and night. Truly, there is no one more possessed than the dispossessed.

The friend, who told Ranbir about the Sikhs, was a refugee himself – from Rawalpindi. His name – Ashish Malhotra.

Seventeen

Upon his arrival in Delhi, Ranbir headed straight for the refugee camp that was located close to the railway station on the grounds of the Red Fort. Why did he go to a refugee camp? Well, quite simply, he needed food and a place to sleep.

Screening was far from careful in these camps, which was quite understandable. Many refugees had little more than their word to identify themselves. Several not even that, just a glassy stare that told the world their former life had been blown out of their minds. It was tough to get bureaucratic in the face of such tragedy and question people about things like missing papers. So there were many like Ranbir – beggars, petty criminals, never-do-wells ... non-refugees that infiltrated refugee camps for food and a place to sleep.

Ranbir registered as a refugee from Lyallpur. One of the first people he met in the camp was Ashish Malhotra. They were billeted in the same tent, with three other men intent on sharing a bottle of country liquor through the night. Ranbir and Ashish, wanting no part of the drinking and unable to sleep, thanks to all the drunken conversation swirling around them, simply lifted their blankets and went outside to sit next to a fire. There they made small talk for a few minutes. Ranbir, not too keen on answering questions about himself, steered the conversation towards Ashish, who was only too happy to talk about himself.

"I'm from Rawalpindi," he began. "My family lived there for over a hundred years, from when it was just a small town, an insignificant dot on the Sikh empire of Ranjit Singh. In front of us it grew into a big city. It was the British who developed Pindi. It was less than 150 miles from the Khyber Pass and, therefore, a perfect place to position a garrison.

"My father was Lala Daulat Ram Malhotra. He owned a general merchant's store in Raja Bazaar, right in the heart of the city. We didn't live in the city, though. We lived in the cantonment area, in Lal Kurti. Our house was a simple two-story structure, four bedrooms in all. We were not rich. But we were comfortable, middle-class.

"I was the youngest. I had two elder brothers. The eldest was a doctor. The one after him helped my father run the store. Me? I had my heart set on the Indian Civil Service.

"I went to Danny's High School for boys. I left at six in the morning, eight during the winter, always one hour before school started. You see it was three miles away and I had to walk. It wasn't until I started college in 1944 that I got a bicycle.

"Ghulam Baksh, Abdul Saeed, Nasir Khan … These were some of my father's friends. You look surprised. These are not Hindu names. Yes, my father had many Muslim friends; so many, in fact, some of our relatives called him a mullah behind his back.

"My father had no fear of partition. True, it meant we would be living in Pakistan, a Muslim state. But Jinnah himself had said that the rights of the Hindus would be protected in Pakistan. Then we had lived in Pindi for generations and, in all that time, we'd had no trouble with the Muslims. They would never harm us. Why, some of them were my father's best friends. We had survived the defeat of Ranjit Singh, the coming and going of the British … We would survive partition as well.

"Then barely a week after independence, on the night of August 23rd, a Muslim mob looted my father's store and burned it to the ground. At its head was one of my father's best friends – Nasir Khan.

"Have you ever seen a man melt? He whittles away bit by bit. Skin rolls off his arms, his legs, his face … Every day you see him he is a little smaller, a little more bent. And then one day you find he has shrunk to nothing. Instead of a man what you have in front of you is a shell. That was my father after that day.

"It was my brother – the eldest one who was a doctor – who decided we had to leave Pindi. The killing and arson were getting worse. The police, that was predominantly Muslim, had gone over to the side of the looters and the fanatics. We were lucky we lived in the cantonment area, where we had the protection of the army. But it was only a matter of time before the army went the way of the police. Already we were hearing stories of Hindu and Muslim soldiers exchanging fire. We simply had to get out.

"My brother tried to sell the house. Nobody would buy it even at half of what it was worth. The people knew we had to leave with or without the money. They knew they only had to wait to occupy it for free.

"We hawked what we could. Still one day before we were to leave, the house was full of things. We could take only so much. My eldest brother decided to burn everything we could not take in the back garden that night. He was damned if he was going to leave anything behind for the looters.

"That night I was the only one to last out the fire. The others all broke down one by one – my mother, my brothers, my sisters-in-law, my nephews and nieces ... They all retreated into the house, where my father, who had by now lost his wits, sat making bird noises. But I stayed behind. Methodical as an undertaker, I fed the last sari, the last toy, the last piece of furniture to the fire. Then I stood back and watched it all burn. I stood there until the last crackle died out and there was nothing left except ashes. Ashes and the smoke oozing out of them. That was when I cried."

He paused, staring fixedly at the black earth. Then he said, looking up, "I guess I don't have to tell you how it feels. You are a refugee, too."

Ranbir didn't say anything. Ashish continued.

"September 11, 1947. The day we left for Delhi. One whole day we sat on the platform waiting for a train. A brute of a day. The heat pressed down on you, almost as if it had you pinned. Even the leaves appeared dead. Not a single one was moving. To make matters worse, there was very little water at the station.

"All day people were fainting, begging for water. There was nothing anyone could do to help. There was no ambulance or first aid. All we could do was pray. At first we prayed for a train. As the day wore, however, we prayed simply for sunset. But when the night came, nobody slept. We were scared, in case a train came or a Muslim mob.

"It seemed every Hindu and Sikh left in Pindi was at the station, strewn all over its platforms, crammed inside its waiting rooms ... With them they had everything they could possibly carry in suitcases, baskets, bedding rolls or simply their hands. As the day progressed, the entire place began to stink. Unable to wait in long queues outside public latrines, people were pissing on the railway tracks, in corners of the platform, any inch of space they could find . . . But no one walked out of the station, not one person, even for a few minutes. They were all scared of missing the train.

'The train came the next morning. The whole place erupted. One moment it was as quiet as a library, with most people much too tired even to converse. The next it had rioted, with people scrambling for the train like a herd of buffaloes gone amok.

"We grabbed what we could and ran, ducking, weaving, wriggling … doing everything we could just to keep moving, always looking for that next inch of daylight, the next bit of space not blocked by a body or a limb. Things fell from our hands. But none of us stopped. Stopping meant you got thrown to the floor and trampled.

"We lost everything we were carrying. Still we were luckier than most. At least we got a compartment. Furthermore, no one was lost, not even my father who had to be virtually hoisted on to the train. There were people who couldn't get inside, who had to cling to the door of the car or climb on top to sit on the hot roof. The stampede at our station was replicated everywhere the train stopped. More and more people bulged out of each car door, or climbed up to sit on top of the train, or clawed for a hold on the compartment windows in a bid to crawl inside. We had to shut our window despite the heat. Already there were more than fifteen people in a compartment meant for four.

"But as the train closed in on the Indian border, you could feel the tension ease. For the first time, people began talking of the lives waiting on the other side. Someone even began to sing.

"Then some fifteen miles from the border, the train stopped.

"Perhaps some Muslims had climbed aboard at one of the

stations and pulled the chain at a pre-ordained spot, or the driver had been bribed to stop the train there. For there were some three hundred Muslims in green shirts, waiting for us with hatchets, swords, clubs and hockey sticks.

"The people hanging on to the doors and windows or clustered on the roof tried to jump off and run. The Muslims, however, chased them down and cut them open or bashed their heads in.

"Several more leaped on to the train. My eldest brother told the children to crouch on the floor. My mother began to pray.

"From other parts of the car came crashes of compartments being broken into, the yells of the killers, the shrieks of their victims ... We could hear people begging for their lives, offering to convert to Islam, offering their wives' jewelry ... In our compartment everyone was praying. Sweat was pouring down our faces. Our lips were moving in unison . . .

"Two bangs, followed by a concerted yell of Allah-o-Akbar, and the compartment door tore from its hinges. My eldest brother was on his feet, screaming we were Muslims, shouting Muslim names, verses from *The Koran* ... But our assailants were not convinced. They stripped him off his trousers and, on seeing he wasn't circumcised, one of them chopped off his penis with a hatchet. Just like that, without a hint of thought, as if he was hacking a dead chicken at the butcher's shop.

"My brother stared at the blood spurting out of him. Then his eyes became huge. He screamed. The man finished him off with a blow to the head.

"Then they turned on the rest of us. Some of us pleaded with them. Others tried to fight. But there was nothing to fight with except bare hands.

"A hockey stick slammed into my shoulder and I fell to the floor. The floor was bloody. I got blood all over my shirt and trousers. Some I smeared on my face. Then I lay face down, as still as I could.

"The killers stayed to make sure everyone was dead and stole everything that wasn't beyond salvage. I held my breath as they turned me over. There was enough blood on my face to convince them. And I guess there was far too much on my shirt and trousers as well. For all they stole from me were my shoes.

"I don't know how long I lay there with my eyes closed. Even after the train started again, I was much too scared to open them in case the killers came back. When I finally got up, it was dark outside and we had crossed the border into India.

"Not only was I the only one alive in the compartment, I was the only one alive in the whole car."

Eighteen

Ashish Malhotra. A young man, not quite twenty-one. Yet a face where lines deep as cracks had broken out; a face etched with drought.

How many kinds of hunger crisscrossed each other on that face? Hunger for food, good health, departed loved ones, a job ... Below all that there was a body shrinking fast. *Have you ever seen a man melt?*

A few spoonfuls of curd, a plateful of rice that was often littered with pebbles ... Some of the cuisine served in the refugee camps. A heavy army blanket, if you were lucky, otherwise, a light blanket or simply a couple of bedsheets with which to get through the cold winter nights. A single tap that catered for thousands of people. With the result, many were forced to wash with water from drains or rainwater lying about in puddles.

No wonder he's always sick, Ranbir thought, looking at Ashish.

In vain he searched for other places to live. The only alternatives were pavements and railway platforms. Everything with a roof demanded money, of which he had little, and he was unable to find any work. So he stayed on in the camp. At least there you got a tent.

To the refugees, he was somewhat of an enigma. They were a people crushed by the weight of tragedy, desperate to share their stories with anyone willing to listen. Ranbir, however, came across as someone who guarded his, as if it were a treasure. Not once did he talk about himself. Even with Ashish, he was primarily a listener. In larger groups, he feigned fatigue, disinterest, even apathy ... any one of several ways to discourage conversation.

However, at all times, he kept his eyes and ears open. With the result, he became a collector of information, swallowing each drop as a drunk might alcohol, preserving it as a curator may an artifact. Consequently, he learned about a local philanthropist who was unique in the sense he distributed free copies of his newspaper in the refugee camps. One Lekhraj Tandon, chief editor of *The Indian Republic*.

January 20, 1948. A time bomb exploded next to the brick wall at the back of Birla House during Gandhi's prayer meeting. The police arrested the man responsible –Madanlal Pahwa – a refugee from Punjab and one of the four men Ranbir had followed in Poona on the night of January 13.

Ranbir learned of the explosion and Pahwa's subsequent arrest around a refugee campfire that night. Ashish and the other refugees there speculated whether Pahwa was simply trying to convey the refugees' displeasure at the release of 550 million rupees to Pakistan, as a result of the Mahatma's fast. Ranbir, however, knew better. The explosion was nothing less than an attempt on the Mahatma's life. He was relieved that only Pahwa had been caught, for Pahwa had only showed up in Poona one week before he left and did not know him personally.

The botched attempt meant Godse and the others were now fugitives. They had to be on their way out of Delhi, if they hadn't gotten out already. And now they had enough on their plate to worry about him.

For the first time in a week, he felt safe.

Two nights later, on January 22nd, around yet another campfire.

"Tandon sahib was here today," a refugee said.

"So what?" another demanded. "He is at some refugee camp practically every day. Thinks by giving us newspapers he can't sell for free he is booking subscribers for the future."

"True," the first one said. "But today was different. He was looking for information on the refugee who set off the bomb at Birla House."

"But wasn't he just protesting the release of the money to the Pakistanis?" Ashish said to the first refugee who had spoken.

"Tandon sahib thinks differently," the refugee said. "He is convinced that it was an attempt on Gandhiji's life. He even offered to pay for the information."

"Really?"

Ashish and the other two refugees continued to converse. Ranbir, however, sat in silence, reflecting on what he had just heard. A newspaper editor was willing to pay for information on Madanlal Pahwa. He'd probably pay more if Ranbir told him that Pahwa was only one of a group of assassins.

But before he paid, the first thing he'd want to know was how Ranbir had gotten his information. And Ranbir didn't know how he'd satisfy him without revealing his role in the Hindu Rashtra Dal.

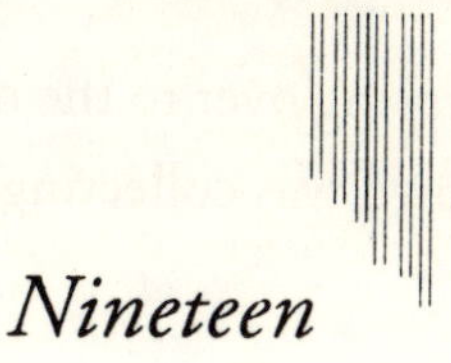

Nineteen

January 30, 1948.

It was just past six in the evening. However, it was already dark. The temperature was plunging. Fires were glowing all over the camp, as people came out of their tents to huddle close to the warmth. Ranbir and Ashish too sat next to a fire. Ashish had a blanket wrapped round him. For the last couple of days, he had been ill. Even now, he was running a fever and coughing constantly. However, he had elected to come out; sitting by a fire was ten times better than freezing in a tent.

Ranbir squatted as close to the fire as he possibly could. His head was bowed. For yet another day, he had been unable to find work. With so many refugees in Delhi, it was hard even to get a menial job. And he needed to find something quick. He was down to his last few rupees.

His thoughts turned to Lekhraj Tandon. Ever since he had learned of his intention to pay for information on Madanlal Pahwa, he had found it hard to get him out of his mind. At times, he was tempted to head straight for the office of *The Indian Republic*. But . . .

"What's happened?" Ashish's voice interrupted his thoughts.

Ranbir looked up to see people hurrying over to the other end of the field. In the distance, a crowd was collecting. He rose to his feet.

"I'll go find out," he said.

He walked over to the other end of the field, where a radio was on. He could faintly make out the voice of an announcer. However, he was unable to get close enough to hear what the announcer was saying. The crowd clustered around the radio was much too thick. Finally, he tapped a man on the shoulder and asked, "What's going on?"

"Gandhiji has been shot dead," the man answered.

The radio revealed few details about the assassination. It had taken place during Gandhi's prayer meeting at Birla House. About the assassin it did not say much, beyond the fact that he was a Hindu. A refugee, Ranbir bumped into, however, claimed to know exactly who he was. He had been at Birla House for that prayer meeting and got a good look at the man. It was the same man, who had been at the refugee camp three days ago, looking for a pistol. His name – Nathuram Godse.

The fact that Godse had been in the camp was news to Ranbir. In fact, if Ranbir hadn't been out looking for work that day, he might well have run into Godse. At the moment, however, he was far too shocked to reflect on his good fortune. The last thing he had expected was for Godse to be in Delhi so soon after the failed attempt of January 20th.

All around him, people were walking about glassy-eyed.

Some were weeping uncontrollably; others were beating their breasts. Less than three weeks ago, when Gandhi fasted on behalf of the Pakistanis, the mantra in the camp had been *Let Gandhi Die*. Even now there were a few men exulting, saying the Mahatma had only got what he deserved. For the most part, however, the tide of sorrow, sweeping the entire nation at the moment, was overrunning the camp as well.

Ranbir slowly made his way back to Ashish. Now that the police had Godse, it wouldn't be long before they found out that Godse headed a Hindu nationalist outfit called the Hindu Rashtra Dal. That would make everyone associated with the Dal a suspect. Unlike Madanlal Pahwa, Godse knew Ranbir well. Why, right that moment, he could be giving his name to the police interrogator.

Ranbir dug in his pockets for a beedi. It was the last one. He had thought he'd save it for later tonight. But he was far too shaken up at the moment. He needed a smoke to calm his nerves.

He reached his campfire to find that it was cold. More than an hour had passed, since he left Ashish. Ashish was coughing, all huddled up in his blanket. Ranbir quickly got the fire going again and gave Ashish his own blanket from inside the tent as well. Then he told him about the assassination. Ashish, still recovering from his bout of coughing, merely nodded. A moment later, he lay down next to the fire to rest a while.

Ranbir smoked his beedi, sitting there, staring at the wavering flame. When he was finished, he threw it away and stretched out on the warm ground beside the fire.

What a mess he had made of his life. Here he was, at twenty-six, down to his last few rupees, with no idea where the next one was coming from. He had no home, no prospects ... What was more, now he probably had the police on his tail as well.

If only he could be someone else . . .

He closed his eyes. He knew he should probably go back inside the tent. But he was much too spent to get up. He decided to simply lie there for a while.

Before he knew it, however, he had dropped off to sleep.

When he woke up, he was shivering all over. The fire was long dead and the sky was gray with the first light of dawn. His clothes were damp with dew. His jaw throbbed, as his teeth bounced off each other. Feverishly, he rubbed his hands together. When they started shaking a little less, he began searching for a match. After finding one, he relit the fire and knelt as close to it as he possibly could. It was a few minutes before he felt somewhat warm. Still kneeling next to the fire, he called out Ashish's name. Ashish was still lying where he had lain down the night before.

When Ashish failed to answer, Ranbir slid over to him and tried shaking him awake. He met with no success. Finally, he turned him over on to his back to catch his breath, as he saw how ashen Ashish's face had become.

He threw the flimsy blankets aside and opened Ashish's shirt to bend down and place his ear to his chest.

He could make out nothing.

Twenty

Like many Indian newspaper editors, Lekhraj Tandon spent the evening of January 30, 1948, closeted with his senior correspondents and staff writers, presiding over rewrite after rewrite in his attempt to insert as much as he could about the assassination in tomorrow morning's edition of his newspaper. It wasn't easy. Information was hard to get and came at a dribble. There was a news blackout in place, as far as the authorities were concerned. Even when Tandon took up the phone himself and called people in government, whom he had known for years, he met with little success. He delayed sending the paper to the printer as long as he could. Finally, however, he could hold off no longer. Reluctantly, he gave his okay and sank exhausted on to the couch in his office. Within minutes, he was asleep.

His peon woke him up, soon after eight in the morning, with a cup of tea. As he drank his tea, Tandon called home and spoke to his wife and daughter. He promised them he'd be home early that day. Sometimes, thanks to the nature of his work, he ended up spending the night in his office. His family was used to that. Yet each time he was forced to do that, he couldn't help feeling a tinge of regret. He loved his family, especially his daughter who had just turned sixteen. In a few years, she'd be ready to get married and go to her husband's house. Once that happened, she'd be her husband's wife, rather than his daughter. So he wanted to spend as much time as he could with her, while she was still in his care. She was, after all, his only child.

After reiterating his promise to be home early, Tandon rang off and went for a wash in the bathroom. Then he returned to his desk, where the morning papers were laid out. As usual, he scanned all the other papers before picking up *The Republic*. When he finally did, his eyes zeroed in on the lead story:

At twenty minutes past five in the evening of January 30th, Gandhiji was shot dead while on his way to his prayer meeting at Birla House. His assassin has been identified as Nathuram Godse...

He stopped at Godse's name and leaned back in his chair to sit with his hands folded and his chin propped up on the end of a thick forefinger. He was a thickset man of five nine. In his early fifties, he was bald, except for a gray patch of hair at the back of his head. He had khaki-colored skin, a thin gray moustache and small astigmatic eyes. His glasses gave him a professorial air. The chaotic nature of his desk, however, where pen and paper were scattered everywhere, and the careless way in which he dressed – his shirt simply hadn't gotten rumpled, it had started out that way when he first put it on almost twenty-four hours earlier – left no one in any doubt as to what he did for a living. He could only be a journalist.

Now he contemplated the lead story in the latest edition of his newspaper with no more satisfaction than when he had read it last night. It was precise and well written, giving a detailed account of exactly what had happened. But Tandon couldn't find one thing there that wasn't replicated in every other front page that morning.

Godse. If only they knew more about Godse.

As it was, they knew very little. The authorities weren't saying a word, beyond the fact that he was a Hindu from Maharashtra, which anyone could figure out from his name. And Tandon's reporters had been unable to dig up much more.

There was a knock on the door. It was the peon, returning to tell Tandon that a refugee had come to see him.

Tandon took a deep breath. Ever since he had let it known he'd be willing to pay for information on Madanlal Pahwa, it seemed just about every starving refugee in Delhi was making a beeline for *The Indian Republic*.

He had half a mind to tell the peon to get rid of the refugee. But he did not. His gut told him this was someone he needed to see. After more than thirty years in journalism, he had learned to listen to his gut.

He told the peon to show the refugee in. The peon came back with Ranbir.

"How do *you* know all this?" Lekhraj Tandon asked Ranbir.

For more than thirty minutes, he had listened with rapt attention, as Ranbir retraced Godse's steps to Poona and told him all about the Hindu Rashtra Dal and the meeting of the four men in the office of the *Hindu Rashtra*, followed by a rendezvous with a man who dressed as a sadhu but was really an arms peddler. Only when Ranbir was finished did he ask his question.

"I met a man who was once in the Hindu Rashtra Dal," Ranbir answered.

"Where?"

"Here in Delhi, yesterday, at the refugee camp at Red Fort."

'This man is a refugee?"

"No, he was only posing as one to get something to eat."

"Why didn't he go to the police with this information?"

"He was scared. Gandhiji had his enemies in the police. Furthermore, if anyone in the Dal ever found out that he had betrayed them to the police, he'd be dead in no time."

"Did you know this man before yesterday?"

"No."

"Then why did he talk to you?"

"He was weak. He hadn't eaten a proper meal in days. He

was coughing and shivering all the time. He had high fever. He needed help, which only I was willing to provide. When he first told me about Godse, I thought he was merely rambling in his fever. But then I heard the authorities had confirmed that Godse was the killer."

"Where is this man now?"

"He is dead. He died in his sleep last night. I found him early this morning."

"What was his name?"

Without any hesitation whatsoever, Ranbir said, "Ranbir Lal."

Tandon wrote down the name on a piece of paper.

"Who was it you said you were?" he asked.

"Ashish Malhotra."

"Where are you from, Ashish?"

"I am from Rawalpindi. My family lived there for over a hundred years, from when it was just a small town, an insignificant dot on the Sikh empire of Ranjit Singh ..."

Part Three

Twenty-one

For over an hour, Munje spoke without interruption, pausing only to sip from a glass of water lying on the table in front of him. He told Ravi about his father's childhood in a Delhi orphanage, his friendship with Aditya Gokhale and subsequent induction in the RSS, the circumstances in which he came to Poona and joined the Hindu Rashtra Dal … He said he had got that information from Ravi's father himself in the four years they had spent together in Poona. Then he went on to talk about those four years, going into detail about the kind of work Ravi's father did for the Hindu Rashtra Dal.

Sapna kept the two men company, leaving the drawing room only to answer the phone. Near the end of the monologue, however, she rose to get her grandfather more water. She returned with a glass of water for Ravi as well.

"I spoke to your father for the last time on the morning of January 13, 1948," Munje was saying. "He was leaving for the newspaper office. My wife had just handed me a list of groceries to get for the house. I was going to be very busy at work that day. So I asked him if he could pick up the groceries on his way home. He said he would. I had little idea then that the next time I'd see him would be in a newspaper more than fifty years later."

He leaned back in the sofa. He was finished. When Sapna handed him his water, he accepted it gratefully and drank up.

Ravi drank his water slowly. He was in a daze. Listening to Ajit Munje talk about his father was like meeting a stranger for the first time. For the man Munje had described was nothing like the father he had known. However, there were now things coming to mind that made it seem all the more plausible. For instance, during a trip to Bombay in 1983, he and his parents had found themselves in a cab with a driver who said he spoke no other language except Marathi. That man was not only taking them round in circles, his cab had a meter that was running faster than usual. His father tried speaking to him in Hindi and English, only to have him shaking his head. Finally, he admonished him in Marathi, which surprised the cab driver so much that he promptly stopped the car and apologized. Ravi and his mother were surprised as well. They didn't know his father could speak Marathi. When his mother asked him where he had learned his Marathi, his father soft-pedaled the issue, saying he had picked up some from a Marathi friend in school. He never told them who that friend was, however, and immediately changed the subject.

"I just wonder who the real Ashish Malhotra was," Munje said, cutting into his thoughts, "or if there was actually one."

"I wouldn't be surprised if there wasn't one," Sapna said. "It's a common enough name."

"No, there was an Ashish Malhotra," Ravi said.

They turned to him.

"When I was twelve, my grandfather told me how he met my father for the first time," Ravi continued. "Like my father, my grandfather was the chief editor of *The Republic* – Lekhraj Tandon.

"After the failed attempt to kill Gandhi on January 20, 1948, my grandfather passed the word in the refugee camps that he was willing to pay for information on Madanlal Pahwa, the refugee who set off the bomb at Birla House on January 20th. As a result, over the next ten days, he was swamped with refugees claiming to have information on Pahwa. Not one, however, had anything he was looking for. On the morning after Gandhi's assassination, however, my father walked into his office with information, not just on Pahwa, but on Godse and the other conspirators as well. When my grandfather asked him how he had come by his information, he said he had got it from a man he had met in the refugee camp at Red Fort. According to my father, the man was simply posing as a refugee to get food and a place to sleep; he had actually been part of the Hindu Rashtra Dal. My father claimed the man was ailing badly when he met him and had died soon afterwards. Before that, however, he had told him everything about Godse, the Hindu Rashtra Dal and the intent to kill

Gandhi. My father had thought he was simply rambling in his fever. It was only after the authorities confirmed that Godse was Gandhi's killer that he took him seriously.

"According to my father, this man's name was Ranbir Lal."

Sapna and Munje exchanged a look.

"You mean that man was really Ashish Malhotra," Munje said.

Ravi nodded.

"Before my grandfather believed my father," he said, "he sent someone to the Red Fort refugee camp to find out if a Ranbir Lal and an Ashish Malhotra were actually registered there. They were. What was more, the records showed that Ranbir Lal had been found dead that morning. Now since my father was Ranbir Lal, the dead man could only be Ashish Malhotra."

Sapna was nodding.

"It's possible," she said. "That winter refugees were dying all the time due to the cold or hunger. The camp officials were shorthanded, with a hundred and one problems to deal with at any given minute. They wouldn't have had the time to check who the dead person was. They would simply have taken your father at his word when he said the dead man was Ranbir Lal.

"In addition, after the assassination the only way your father could have been sure that he was safe from the police was by killing Ranbir Lal. For after Godse was arrested, anyone even remotely associated with him was a suspect. That included just about everybody in the Hindu Rashtra Dal. But in the case of your father, even if someone came looking for him, they would be unlikely to pursue him after learning he was dead. So he had every reason to tell the camp officials that the dead man was Ranbir Lal."

There was a short pause. Then Munje said, "The article, that appeared in the newspaper when your father retired, said he began his career at *The Republic* in 1948, as an *office boy*."

"Yes, that's right," Ravi said. "After my grandfather heard my father's story about how his entire family had been massacred on the train over to Delhi from Rawalpindi, he wanted to do all he could to help him. You see my grandfather was originally from west Pakistan. Then he had lost family in the riots accompanying partition as well. He realized what my father really needed was a regular source of income, which could only come from a job. Whatever little money he got in exchange for information would come and go in no time. So he offered him the position of an office boy."

He added, with a shake of the head, "Now, of course, we know that my father was no refugee. So the story he told my grandfather was probably Ashish Malhotra's, as well.

"Anyway, my father worked as an office boy for the next three years. He told me later that those were the years in which he actually learned his English. Until then, it was his weakest language. He could understand it all right. But since leaving school he hadn't used it much, I guess, other than writing brief notes such as this one."

He motioned towards the biography of Srinivas Ramanujam that still lay on the table before continuing.

"*The Republic*, however, was an English-language newspaper. Its writers, editors, proofreaders, photographers ... just about everyone over the rank of office boy thought and conversed in English. Then, as part of his duties, my father was often called upon to type a letter in English or take a message over the phone from someone who spoke no other language fluently. Therefore, soon after he started at *The Republic*, my father realized it would be in his best interests to improve his English. So he began working on it. By 1951 he was more than competent, in speaking as well as writing English."

"I'm not surprised," Munje said. "If your father could master Marathi, English wouldn't have been so difficult. Unlike Marathi, at least he had a background in English. It was the medium of instruction in his school."

"How did he go from office boy to journalist?" Sapna asked.

"Well, in 1951 there was an opening for a junior reporter at *The Republic*. My father approached my grandfather for it, who decided to give it to him."

"I read that in the article that appeared in the newspaper when he retired," Munje said. "And what I couldn't figure out was how your grandfather gave him the chance. By hiring your father as a journalist, your grandfather was moving someone from the blue-collar world to the white collar. He was asking people to work side by side with someone who only yesterday they had considered beneath them. That was bound to cause resentment. So why did your grandfather do it? Surely your parents were not married at the time?"

"No, my parents didn't get married until 1954. They didn't even meet until 1953. No, what tipped the scales in my father's favor was the fact that my grandfather was an outsider himself. He came from a small town, which is now in Pakistan. He had bucked the odds by beating out all the big-city boys to become the chief editor of a national daily. Since he had come up the hard way, in my father he saw a bit of himself. Then he had lost family and property, including his ancestral home, during partition. So he had genuine sympathy for someone like my father, who he believed came from a background similar to his own and had lost everything during partition.

"Therefore, despite his misgivings, he decided to give him the chance. My father grabbed it with both hands. By 1953 he had more than repaid my grandfather's faith in him. He was a bright young star at *The Republic*. Great things were expected from him. That was when my grandfather introduced him to my mother. They were married a year later."

"The early 1950's would be the right time for someone like your father to come out of hibernation," Sapna said. "Godse was hanged in 1949, as was Apte. Of the others, arrested in connection with the assassination, only Savarkar was let off due to lack of evidence. The rest were languishing in prison and likely to do so for a long time. Even Savarkar no longer wielded the kind of influence he had before the assassination. The Hindu Rashtra Dal had been smashed. The RSS, though no longer banned, was struggling to find its feet. It would be years before it was a force again. Most importantly, with Gandhi's killers punished and the movement in disarray, the Hindu nationalists were no longer the prime target of the security forces. Therefore, your father could feel reasonably safe, knowing his former comrades in the Hindu nationalist movement were grappling with their own problems to worry about him, while the security forces had no interest in his past whatsoever.

"Then he had a new name and was in the print media. He might have faced more of a danger of being exposed in television. But there was no television in India in the 1950's. Furthermore, your father joined the English press. There was a fair Hindu nationalist presence in the Hindi press or at any of the vernacular newspapers. But English is the language of the urban middle-class and the elite. And in the 1950's there were few Hindu nationalists in their ranks. So all in all, your father made his move at the right time."

Munje nodded in agreement. Ravi leaned back, marveling at everything he had learned about his father that evening. Not in his wildest dreams could he have thought that possible. He shook his head.

"To think all these years I didn't know the first thing about my father," he said, "not even his name. If it wasn't so pathetic, it would actually be funny."

"Don't be harsh, Ravi," Munje said. "After the assassination, there were so many times when I would have given anything to be someone else. I didn't have the slightest idea about the plot to kill Gandhi. But that didn't matter one bit. The police arrested me because I was a member of the Hindu Rashtra Dal. They believed, on that basis, I had to be part of the conspiracy. I lost my job soon after I was arrested and had to prove my innocence in court. Finally, I was exonerated. But even that didn't help matters. People called me a murderer to my face. They were just as bad to my wife and daughter. We were forced to leave Poona. I tried to make a new life for us in Bombay. But even there the past caught up with me. Finally, we left Maharashtra and came to Delhi. Even here I was like a man in hiding. For years I kept my head down and didn't breathe a word about my life in Poona to anyone. Even Sapna got to know about it only recently, and that, too, because one day she came home from the university and told me she had discovered that someone with my name had been part of the Hindu Rashtra Dal. She was determined to find out more about that person. That was when I decided it was time to make a clean breast of things."

"When he first told me I couldn't believe it," Sapna said. "The last thing I could have thought was that my grandfather was a part of the Hindu Rashtra Dal."

"You kept that picture my father and you took with Godse all these years," Ravi said to Munje.

"I thought I had got rid of it long ago," Munje said. "When we left Poona, I disposed off everything that even remotely connected me to Gandhi's assassins. However, when I told Sapna about my days in the Dal, she wanted to know if I had retained anything from those days – pictures, letters, old copies of the *Hindu Rashtra* … I didn't think I had anything. However, I emptied out all my old trunks, just in case. There I found the book on Srinivas Ramanujam that was presented by your father. As I dusted it off, the picture fell out."

Ravi picked up the book that was still lying on the drawing room table.

"You liked to read about mathematicians," he said.

"Well, I was a mathematics teacher myself," Munje said. "So I guess it was only natural."

"What did my father like to read?"

"Nonfiction mostly."

At least that hadn't changed over the years.

"We were all different," Munje continued. "Godse, for instance, liked mysteries. He even got Aditya Gokhale hooked on them. God, what a fan of Perry Mason he was."

Ravi started.

"Perry Mason!" he said.

"Yes," Sapna said. "In fact, the last book Godse ever read was a Perry Mason novel, on the night before he killed Gandhi."

Ravi stared at her. The Perry Mason novel, his father had seen on Rashmi's desk, was a secondhand book.

Could it be?

"What's the matter, Ravi?" Sapna asked.

Ravi told them.

"Where's that book now?" Munje wanted to know.

"My father didn't have time to give it back," Ravi said. "So it must be in the bookcase in his study. That's where he kept all his books."

Twenty-two

Ravi's father's study was located to the front of the house, next to the drawing room. At twelve by ten, it was the smallest room in the house. Compared to the other rooms, it was bare. When Ravi's father was editor-in-chief of *The Indian Republic*, it had been positively spartan. Then the only pieces of furniture it held were the desk and the steel bookcase that stood in front of the wall, across the room from the desk. However, after Ravi's father quit as editor-in-chief and exchanged his large office for a columnist's cubicle, his steel filing cabinet and the various citations he had received for journalistic excellence had come home to the study. The filing cabinet now stood beside the desk, while the citations adorned the walls. The floor, however, continued to be uncarpeted.

In Ravi's mind, the study embodied his father more than any other room in the house. Just like him, it was spare and to the point. It was the only room in the house that he had furnished. The rest of it had been furnished by his mother.

The bookcase was large, with four rows of shelves. The books were stocked in no obvious order. There were paperbacks squeezed in between hardcover books, histories placed next to biographies … Ravi, however, assumed that since the book didn't belong to his father, it was probably in the top shelf, which was at eye level. His father would want to keep a book, he'd have to eventually return, where he could get it easily.

He was right. The book was right in the middle of the top shelf, sandwiched between *All the President's Men* and Naipaul's *Among the Believers*. It was a slim book, which had started out as a paperback. Its age, however, had necessitated the black binding. Ravi picked it off the shelf and opened it. Sapna and Munje, who had accompanied him home, looked over his shoulder.

The three of them didn't have to look far. On the first page itself, there was a note written in blue ink with a fountain pen:

To Aditya with warm regards.

Nathuram

Poona, March 5, 1947

The three of them stood in silence, transfixed by the note. Finally, Sapna spoke, simply confirming what they already knew.

"This was written by Godse," she said. "I have seen samples of his handwriting. This is him all right."

Ravi was still staring at the note. It certainly explained why his father was so exercised when he picked up the book in Rashmi's office.

"The last time I saw Aditya was in Poona in August, 1947," Munje said. "He was leaving for Punjab to organize the Hindus against Muslim gangs. Is it possible that he's still alive?"

"Where did Rashmi get this book?" Sapna asked Ravi.

"She said it was in a bookshop in R.K. Puram called …"

He paused, as he tried to remember. Then it came to him.

"Popular Book Depot," he said.

"R.K. Puram is huge," Sapna said. "Did she tell you in which sector this bookshop is located?"

Ravi shook his head. She had, however, written down the exact location for his father. If his father had gone there …

He turned and called out for Hari Singh, telling him to get Suresh. Presently Suresh appeared. He was a slim man, in his mid-twenties, dressed in a white chauffeur's uniform. He came in, hat in hand, the concern on his face indicating he was wondering why he had been summoned.

"Suresh," Ravi said. "Did you take my father to a bookshop in R.K. Puram called the Popular Book Depot?"

"Yes, sahib," Suresh answered. "We went there two days ago."

"Do you remember where exactly it's located?"

"Yes, sahib. It's in the R.K. Puram Sector 6 market."

Sapna glanced at her watch.

"It's just past nine," she said. "Shops in R.K. Puram generally stay open late. Then today's a Friday night. There's a good chance the shop will still be open. If we leave right away, we'll be there in ten minutes."

"Let's go," Ravi said.

The car was standing in the driveway. The three of them got in the back. Soon they were underway. Ravi told Suresh to step on the gas. He had no idea what he had learned about his father so far that day had to do with his murder. But he felt he was getting closer to cracking the puzzle.

They were in the market's parking lot in less than ten minutes. The market was housed in a single-story building, rectangular in shape, with shops on all four sides. The Popular Book Depot was right in the middle of the line of shops facing south. It was a small bookshop that sold all kinds of secondhand books. Ravi was glad he had told Suresh to step on the gas. For when they reached the shop, it was about to close. Its shutter was already half the way down.

Ravi and Sapna ducked under the shutter to enter the shop. Munje said he'd wait outside. His back wouldn't let him bend down that much.

The only person present in the shop was a short, thickset man, with a fleshy, cleanshaven face. He was dressed in blue trousers and a short-sleeved madras shirt. He was standing behind the cash register and counting the day's take. Ravi headed straight for him and showed him the book. The man took one look at it and nodded.

"Yes, I know this book," he said. "Just two days ago someone brought it in and asked me how I got it."

"Was this man old, possibly in his seventies?" Ravi asked.

"Yes."

That must have been his father.

"What did you tell him?" he asked the man.

"What he wanted to know. I had nothing to hide. I bought this book ten days ago from a servant boy called Kishan who worked in one of the flats in Sector 6."

"A servant boy?"

"Yes, he was a Nepali. He had just got word that his mother was ill. He was going home to Nepal to be with her. To get there he needed money. He had five books to sell. This was the only one I wanted. The others were all about Hindu nationalism. There was no way I could have sold them."

Ravi and Sapna glanced at each other. Then Sapna said, "You said this boy Kishan worked as a servant?"

"Yes," the man said.

"Did he know English?"

The man laughed.

"Of course not," he said. "He was a servant boy."

"Then what was he doing with an English-language book like this one?" Sapna asked. "Surely he didn't buy it."

The man shrugged his shoulders.

"I don't know how he got it," he said. "I had no reason to ask him."

And why should he ask? Ravi thought. He would have known the book was probably stolen; the desperate act of a poor boy doing all he could to get back to his ailing mother as soon as possible. That would have been enough for him to drive as hard a bargain as he possibly could with the boy. Chances were, he had got the book for next to nothing.

Ravi wanted to get out of the shop as quickly as he could. If he lingered a little longer, he feared he might lose his temper.

"Where is Kishan now?" he asked the man.

"I don't know. Somewhere in Nepal, I guess."

"Which flat did he work in?'

The man smiled and reached under the table for a notebook.

"I made sure I wrote that down," he said. "Can't trust boys like that, uneducated and a Nepali to boot. Who knows he might have stolen that book? Had to do some arm-twisting to get it out of him, though. Only when I threatened to call the police did he come up with the answer."

Ravi gritted his teeth. Sapna placed her hand on his arm. The man looked up from his notebook.

"Flat C-16," he said.

Twenty-three

Like other flats in R.K. Puram, flat number C-16 was housed in a dull yellow, two-story building that contained four flats in all – two on the ground floor and two upstairs. C-16 was an upstairs flat, situated in one of the bylanes of R.K. Puram. Ordinarily, it would have been hard to find in the dark. Suresh, however, was able to get them there in no time. He said he had taken Ravi's father there two days ago.

According to Suresh, Ravi's father had gone there straight from the bookshop. He had spent about an hour upstairs, before coming down in the company of a tall, thin young man dressed in a kurta-pajama. The young man had walked him to the car, where the two said goodbye.

That was all Suresh could tell them. He didn't know who that young man was. Sapna, however, reasoned that if indeed he lived in that flat, either he worked for the government or was related to someone who did. R.K. Puram was a neighborhood that housed government servants.

When they reached C-16, however, they found the flat dark. In vain, they pressed the doorbell. Finally, they went downstairs to look at the mailbox. There was no name on it, simply the address.

They were wondering whether they should talk to the people who lived in the neighboring flats, when they heard a footfall in the stairs. It was a young girl in her mid-teens. The cheap salwar kameez she had on indicated she was a servant girl, possibly on her way home after completing the day's work. Ravi called her over.

"You work in flat C-14?" he asked.

C-14 was the other upstairs flat in the building.

"Yes, sahib," the girl said.

"Do you know who lives in C-16?"

"I have seen two men – one young, one old."

"Old? How old?" Munje asked.

"About your age, sahib."

Ravi and Munje glanced at each other. The same thought was crossing both their minds. Could that man be Aditya Gokhale?

"When was the last time you saw them?" Sapna asked the girl.

"Early yesterday morning when I was coming to work. They were leaving in their Ambassador car."

Ravi caught his breath. His father had been run over by an Ambassador.

"What color was this Ambassador?" he asked.

"White."

That Ambassador had also been white.

"What are their names?" Munje asked the girl.

"Their last name is Puri. The Nepali boy, who used to work there, told me the old man is simply called Baba, while the young man is Vinayak."

"How long have they been in the flat?" Ravi asked.

"Not long. Only about three weeks."

"What does Puri sahib do?'

"He is supposed to be a police officer."

Ravi stared at the girl. The S.H.O. of the Vasant Vihar police station was also called Puri. Could it be the same person?

The servant girl could tell them nothing more. After she was gone, Ravi said, "The car that killed my father was a white Ambassador."

"It could be a coincidence," Sapna said. "There are plenty of white Ambassadors around."

"The name of the S.H.O. of the Vasant Vihar police station is also Puri."

Sapna shrugged her shoulders. "It's a common name," she said.

Munje, apparently nonplussed by the whole conversation, was looking from one to the other.

"If you want we can confirm whether this Puri is actually the S.H.O. Puri you are talking about," Sapna said. 'One of my colleagues at the university is married to an Assistant Commissioner of Police. He works out of the same police district headquarters building that contains the Vasant Vihar police station. I have their phone number at home. I could give them a call and ask her husband. He should know where the S.H.O. lives."

"Let's do it," Ravi said.

They went back to her flat, which was little over a mile away. On the way, Ravi asked Sapna about her colleague. Sapna said her name was Anita Prasad. She was a research scholar in ancient Indian history. She had gotten married a year ago. She and her husband Mohit lived in Moti Bagh.

Soon they were outside Sapna's flat. They made their way upstairs. Sapna started to go to her room for the phone number. Munje, however, told her to wait. He hadn't said a word since Ravi had mentioned that his father was run over by a white Ambassador.

"All right," he said, turning to Ravi. "Now tell me what's going on?"

"What do you mean?" Ravi asked.

"Well, first I thought you simply wanted to learn about your father. But then you brought up the book, after which we ran about trying to find Aditya Gokhale. I didn't say anything then. I guess I was far too keen to see Aditya. But then, out of nowhere, you bring up the fact that your father was run over by a white Ambassador. Then you begin talking about the S.H.O of the Vasant Vihar police station. So clearly there is much more to this than I thought. I want to know what it is."

"Ravi believes his father was murdered," Sapna said.

"What?" Munje said.

Ravi nodded.

"Why do you think that?" Munje asked him.

Ravi recounted everything he had learned from Atma Ram. When he was finished, Munje wanted to know if he had talked to the police. Ravi gave an account of his phone conversation with the head constable at the Vasant Vihar police station. At the end of it, Munje said, "If A.S.I. Kapil's duty ended at four then what was he doing investigating a case in the evening? Then, if he had been sent to investigate the case, why was the case taken away from him and that, too, in less than a day?"

"I wondered about that myself," Ravi said.

"The only language policemen in this country understand is influence from the top," Munje said. "You'll have to bring plenty of that to bear if you want them to catch your father's murderer. Sapna's colleague's husband should be able to help you there."

"I'll just go and call them," Sapna said.

She rose to go to her room. Ravi and Munje stayed back in the drawing room. The old man looked preoccupied, obviously turning over everything he had just learned in his mind. Ravi leaned back in his chair. He was exhausted. He couldn't believe he had been in Delhi for less than twenty-four hours. Right now his life in America seemed light years away.

He was certain his father had met Aditya Gokhale in flat C-16. Otherwise, he wouldn't have spent an hour in there as Suresh claimed. After meeting him, the very next morning he had called Rashmi at *The Indian Republic* and asked for the clipping of a story, she had done more than two years ago, on a Hindu nationalist outfit called the Hindu Tigers.

Was there a connection between his father's meeting with Aditya Gokhale and his request for that particular story?

"Would Aditya Gokhale still be involved in the Hindu nationalist movement, even after all these years?" he asked Munje.

"I would think so," Munje said. "Aditya ate, drank and slept Hindu nationalism. Of everyone I knew in the Hindu Rashtra Dal, there was no one more committed than him."

"Not even Godse?"

"No. Godse liked to talk. He had all kinds of grand plans. But when the time to act came, he rarely came up with the goods. Gandhi's assassination was the only time he followed anything to its logical conclusion. Aditya, however, was a doer. He didn't say much. But if there was a scrap, you could be sure that Aditya would be right in the thick of things. In 1947 everyone in the Dal was talking about going to Punjab and fighting on behalf of the Hindus there. The only one who actually went was Aditya. And he never said he was going until he had bought his train ticket."

Sapna entered the room, with a cordless phone in hand.

"It took me a while to get through," she said. "The line was engaged. I just caught them. They were about to turn the ringer off and go to bed. Anyway, Mohit says that Puri lives in Vasant Kunj. However, he wants to talk to you. I told him you believe your father was murdered. He wants to help."

Ravi took the phone from her.

"Hello," he said.

"Hello, Ravi," the voice was deep, almost a baritone. "I'm really sorry about your father. I used to love reading him in the newspaper. Sapna says you think that he was murdered."

"Yes."

"Why don't you come by my office on Monday. I'll have Puri come in as well and we'll see what we can do. I'd see you sooner, but we've got our hands full with Musharraf's visit this weekend."

"Thanks, Mohit," Ravi said. 'Listen, have you heard of a group called the Hindu Tigers?"

There was a short pause. Then Mohit said, "What about the Hindu Tigers?"

"Yesterday morning my father called *The Republic* and requested the clipping of a story about them. Just the evening before, after more than fifty years, he had met an old friend who had once been involved with the Hindu nationalist movement and probably still is. I was wondering if there was a connection between the two."

"Your father met this friend in Delhi?"

"Yes."

"Do you have the clipping he requested?"

"Yes, I have it at home."

"Where do you live?"

"40 Poorvi Marg. That's in Vasant Vihar."

"I'll meet you there in half an hour."

Twenty-four

Mohit was a lanky man in his late twenties. He had short black hair, cut close to the scalp, a broad forehead, dark eyes and a light moustache arching on top of a wide mouth. He had grown up in Delhi. When he spoke, however, at times, his Bihari roots crept into his voice. For instance, when he conversed in English, the 'sh' sounds often came out as 's' sounds.

That night he was wearing jeans and a short-sleeved blue shirt. He had clearly dressed in a hurry, putting on whatever came readily to hand. The shirt, as well as the jeans, was well worn and badly wrinkled.

When he arrived at Ravi's house, Hari Singh showed him into the drawing room. There Ravi, Sapna and Munje were waiting for him. Mohit said hello to Sapna who introduced him to Ravi and her grandfather. Mohit folded his hands and said namaste to Munje. Then he shook hands with Ravi who asked him to sit down. He settled in an overstuffed chair, politely refusing Ravi's offer of tea or coffee and asked to see the clipping.

Ravi handed it to him. Mohit glanced at the picture that showed five protesters, all young men, with placards. Then he leaned back to read the story. When he was done, he looked up and said, "This is just a straightforward story about a protest held more than two years ago."

Ravi nodded.

"You said you were wondering if this story was somehow connected to an old friend your father met the day before," Mohit said. "Is this friend mentioned anywhere in the story?"

"No," Ravi said.

"What about the picture?" Mohit asked.

Ravi took a look at it.

"No, these men are far too young," he said. "My father's friend would now be in his seventies and ..."

He broke off in mid-sentence. He had just remembered something. One more time, he studied the picture. Then he called Hari Singh and told him to get Suresh quick.

"What's the matter, Ravi?" Sapna asked.

"I just want to clear something up," Ravi said.

Suresh entered the room.

"Suresh," Ravi said, "you told me that when my father came down after visiting that flat in R.K. Puram he was accompanied by a young man."

"Yes, sahib."

"Did you get a good look at this man's face?"

"Yes, sahib."

Ravi handed him the clipping.

"Do you see him anywhere in this picture?" he asked.

Suresh gazed at the picture. After a brief pause, he said, "That's him."

He pointed to a slim, cleanshaven man, standing in the middle of the picture.

According to the caption below the picture, the man's name was Ganesh Dhawan. He appeared to be in his mid-to-late twenties. His hair was cut, like a soldier, in the shortest of crew cuts. He was wearing a headband that had to be saffron, even though it didn't show in the black and white photo. He had an angular face, deepset eyes and a sharp nose. His mouth was open; the camera had caught him in the act of shouting a slogan. He was wearing trousers and a long-sleeved sweater. The front collars of a shirt peeked out, just below his neck, from underneath the sweater. In his right hand, he held a placard that read PAKISTANIS ONLY LEARN FROM KICKS.

Mohit fired off a burst of questions at Suresh. Did Dhawan say anything to Ravi's father? Did he give or receive anything from him? Had Suresh seen him since then? ... Suresh appeared dazed by the onslaught. He could add little to what he had already told Ravi. Dhawan, he said, simply walked Ravi's father to the car, where he said goodbye by folding his hands in a namaste. Ravi's father acknowledged the greeting. Then the two men went their separate ways.

After Suresh, to his apparent relief, was dismissed, Ravi said to Mohit, "It's clear you're not here because of my father's murder. So tell me, what's going on?"

Mohit took a deep breath. Then he said, "Ganesh Dhawan is a hardcore Hindu nationalist. He has a record of arrests as long as your arm. He has been in and out of jail since he was an eighteen-year-old in 1992. Each one of those arrests was related to some Hindu nationalist cause or other – the construction of the Ram temple, banning cow slaughter, religious conversions ...

"Dhawan comes from Gurdaspur in Punjab. He was raised in an ashram there. He is an orphan. He started out in the RSS as a boy. Over the years, however, he drifted towards more radical organizations like the Shiv Sena and the Bajrang Dal. He became especially active in their goon squads. When he wasn't courting arrest during an agitation, he was ransacking card shops on Valentine's Day, or clashing with Muslim goons or those from rival political parties like the Congress and the communists. That's how he spent most of the nineties.

"In 1999, however, Dhawan split from the mainstream of the Hindu nationalist movement. The split was caused by Prime Minister Vajpayee's peace initiative with Pakistan. Like other Hindu nationalists, Dhawan had high hopes from Vajpayee. Vajpayee, after all, was a Hindu nationalist himself. However, Vajpayee, much to his shock, made a peace overture to Pakistan. For a hardcore Hindu nationalist like Dhawan, who believes passionately in restoring the integrity of undivided India, that amounted to sacrilege.

"With a handful of other like-minded radicals, Dhawan formed the Hindu Tigers on the eve of the P.M.'s visit to Pakistan in 1999. One of the prime aims of that organization is to unite the country, as they say. In the beginning, they stuck to conventional political activity. They opened an office in Gurdaspur, put out a weekly newspaper, participated in protests and agitations ... Over the past year, however, they have become increasingly militant. Nine months ago they roughed up a newspaper editor for arguing too passionately for a dialogue with Pakistan. And just three months ago a communist party worker was shot dead in Gurdaspur. The police there believed that Dhawan was behind the shooting. But they didn't have the proof to prosecute him.

"When this weekend's Indo-Pak summit was announced in May, we were apprehensive as to what Dhawan and his cohorts would do. After all, they had opposed the first summit in 1999. Since that summit the Pakistanis had sent infiltrators into Kashmir, culminating in the Kargil war. So from their standpoint, this summit would represent an even bigger sellout than the last one. Furthermore, any peace with Pakistan goes against their goal of restoring the integrity of undivided India.

'But all they did was condemn the summit in their newspaper. There was no frantic activity, no attempt to mobilize people, nothing the least bit remarkable. We were gratified. If all the Hindu Tigers were going to do was make some noise, then we had nothing to fear.

"Then three weeks ago Dhawan disappeared. The police in Gurdaspur had him under observation. He gave them the slip and vanished off the face of the earth. We questioned his fellow members in the Hindu Tigers. They could tell us nothing. Nor could any of our undercover people. In fact, the first I heard that he was in Delhi was right now.

"I can now see why we were unable to locate him. He was hiding out in government housing, that, too, in a flat supposed to be assigned to a police officer. That's the last place where anyone would think of looking for him. Then he was also using an assumed name.

"The question now, however, is why did he go to such lengths to conceal himself? Is he planning to disrupt this summit? If so, how?"

Twenty-five

Mohit excused himself to use the phone. Sapna, obviously worn out after a long day, asked for a cup of coffee. No sooner than she spoke, Ravi realized how hungry he was. They had all missed dinner. It was far too late for dinner now. However, he called Hari Singh and told him to rustle up some coffee and sandwiches.

Everything was a lot clearer now. Given his memory for faces, a bell would have gone off in his father's head the instant he laid eyes on Ganesh Dhawan. He probably didn't place him immediately, possibly not until the next morning when he called Rashmi for the story. His gut, however, would have told him that he knew that face. That realization would have prompted him to attempt to pinpoint it. To that end, he would have probed Dhawan through a series of searching questions. That would have been enough to scare Dhawan and his companion who, in all probability, was Aditya Gokhale. If they were indeed lying low, then the last thing they would want was a journalist snooping about.

Apparently, his father had thrown quite a scare into them. Not only had they abandoned the flat, they had ended up killing him. They had waited for him outside his house and when he came out to make the call from the public telephone booth, they had run him over with their car and made their escape.

Yes, that was how it must have happened. The question, however, was that what was it that Dhawan and Gokhale had in mind that they were willing to commit murder to stay incognito. And in the case of Gokhale, the murder victim was actually a long-lost boyhood friend.

Then there were still question marks as to how the police were handling the investigation.

Hari Singh arrived with the coffee and sandwiches. Munje, who had been immersed in his own thoughts ever since Mohit had finished telling them about Dhawan and the Hindu Tigers, indicated he didn't want anything. Sapna, much too tired and hungry to try and cajole him, did not insist. Instead, she joined Ravi in partaking the sandwiches and coffee.

Mohit returned to the room, saying he had made a few calls in his bid to find out who exactly had been assigned flat C-16. Finally, he had been able to locate the right person. Now the man was on his way to his office to look at the files. Once he called with the information, they would know whom to question about Dhawan's intentions. They may even get a clue as to his current whereabouts. Until then, the only thing they could do was wait. The wait wouldn't be long, though, since the man lived close to his office.

For the next few minutes, the room was silent. Ravi and Sapna concentrated on eating, while Mohit paced impatiently. Munje sat still, staring straight ahead.

It was Munje who finally broke the silence.

"You say this Ganesh Dhawan comes from Gurdaspur," he said to Mohit.

"Yes."

"And he's an orphan."

"Yes."

"Who raised him?'

"He was raised in an ashram in Gurdaspur that looks after orphaned boys. In fact, his political views were probably shaped over there. The ashram has a distinct Hindu nationalist bent. The day-to-day activities, the curriculum followed in its school ... Everything is heavily influenced by it. Dhawan still maintains close ties to it. In fact, it is widely believed the money for the Hindu Tigers comes from the ashram. Certainly a lot of its recruits do."

"Is this ashram affiliated to any Hindu nationalist organization?"

"No, it's entirely independent."

"Then where does the money to run it come from?"

"From contributions made by Hindu refugees that settled down in Gurdaspur after partition. They have supported it from the beginning. Many of them are dead. Their descendants, however, continue the support. Some of them have moved out of Gurdaspur. A few have even gone abroad. Yet they still make donations."

"Who is in charge of the ashram?"

"Until May it was the same man who founded it. Last month, however, I heard that he had handed over the reins to a successor. I don't know the successor too well. The old man, however, was much revered in that community. I believe he made quite a name for himself during partition, helping a number of refugees escape across the border to Gurdaspur. He set up the ashram in the 1950's. He began small, with a few contributions from refugee families. Then as the refugees settled down and began to prosper, their contributions grew and so did the ashram. Right now it's spread over twenty-five acres."

"Is this man also a refugee from Pakistan?"

"No. Actually, it's rather interesting. He's not even Punjabi, although he speaks the language fluently. He's from Maharashtra."

Ravi and Sapna paused while eating.

"What is his name?" Munje asked Mohit.

"Aditya Gokhale."

The phone rang. Mohit left the room to answer it. After he was gone, Munje said, "When he mentioned that Dhawan comes from a town in Punjab, I began to wonder if Dhawan and Aditya were somehow connected. After all, Punjab was where Aditya went in 1947. Chances were he would have stayed on there after the assassination. At the time, there could be no better place for a devout Hindu nationalist like him. With so many Hindu refugees coming over the border from Pakistan, there was bound to be plenty of goodwill. Then, given all the turmoil in the state due to partition, there was very little law. Furthermore, Aditya had spent a number of years in North India in his youth. He spoke both Hindi and Punjabi fluently.

"Then I was also intrigued by the name that Ganesh was using – Vinayak. In Maharashtra Vinayak is another name for Lord Ganesh. In addition, it was the first name of Savarkar and the middle name of Godse. Aditya admired both those men. The fact he kept the book that Godse presented him all these years means he still does."

"Why would he want to kill my father?" Ravi asked.

"That I have no idea."

Mohit returned to the room. He appeared preoccupied, as he stepped over to a chair and sat down heavily. Ravi, Sapna and Munje waited expectantly. Mohit, however, remained silent. Finally, it was Ravi who asked him, "Did he tell you who the flat is assigned to?"

Mohit glanced at him.

"Yes," he said. "It's S.H.O. Puri, which I find hard to believe. I couldn't attend his daughter's marriage last night. But I could swear the RSVP was a flat in Vasant Kunj. I also don't remember his request for government accommodation ever clearing my desk. However, it is possible that I signed off on it and forgot all about it. Such a request, after all, is a routine matter. But the way this particular one was handled is certainly not routine. It originated on May 28th and the flat was allotted in less than a month. That is impossible in the normal course, given the bureaucracy and the number of people queuing up for government accommodation. Someone with influence had to intervene on Puri's behalf."

"You said the request for accommodation originated on May 28th?" Sapna said.

"Yes," Mohit answered.

"Wasn't the Indo-Pak summit announced round that time?"

"Yes, it was. Actually, it was officially announced five days earlier – on May 23rd."

Twenty-six

Mohit said he was going to the S.H.O.'s flat. He called for backup, telling a sub-inspector to meet him with a detachment of constables in Vasant Kunj. Ravi said he was coming with him. Mohit tried to talk him out of it. Ravi, however, told him it was *his* father who had been murdered. That shut Mohit up. However, he said there was no way he would let Sapna and Munje come along. If Puri was indeed harboring Dhawan, there was every chance of things getting out of hand.

Sapna said that she and her grandfather would go home and wait to hear from Ravi. She made Ravi promise that he'd give them a call and let them know how things went, no matter how late the hour. Before leaving, both she and Munje asked Ravi to be careful.

Ravi and Mohit made their way to Vasant Kunj in Mohit's car. On the way, Ravi quizzed Mohit about Puri.

"Is he a Hindu nationalist?" he asked.

"Not that I know of," Mohit answered. "In fact, he always struck me as someone who wasn't much into politics. That's why I can't figure out his involvement with Dhawan."

"What surprises me is the fact that he's marrying his daughter off at the same time."

"Well, the date for the marriage was set well before the summit was announced. Actually, I told him to put off the wedding once the dates for the summit came out. I figured he'd have trouble getting leave. He told me he couldn't do that. Apparently the boy works in Dubai and this is the only time he can come for at least a year. Like I thought, Puri did have trouble getting leave, a lot of trouble. In fact, if the Deputy Commissioner of Security hadn't intervened on his behalf, I very much doubt if he could have swung it."

Ravi was quiet for a moment, thinking over what Mohit had just told him. Then he said, "I don't work in India. But a Deputy Commissioner going out of his way for an S.H.O. who is no more than an inspector-level officer ... That does sound a bit out of the ordinary."

Mohit glanced at him.

"The two of them are close friends," he said.

"How come?" Ravi asked. "A Deputy Commissioner is so much higher in rank. Then he's probably better educated and comes from a much more affluent background. Such a friendship would be rare in America. In a society as hierarchical as India, it is impossible to imagine."

Mohit hesitated. Then he said, "Sometimes life takes a turn that makes all that irrelevant.

"Puri had a son, Abhay. Abhay was in the army. During the Kargil war in 1999, Abhay's unit was ambushed by the Pakistanis. Not a single man survived. Commanding that unit was none other than Deputy Commissioner Sethi's son, Mahesh.

"Abhay and Mahesh were only sons. So their loss hit their fathers especially hard. The grief they shared brought them together. With the result, they became close, despite the difference in status."

There was a short pause. Then Ravi said, "Do you think the Deputy Commissioner used his influence to get Puri the flat?"

Mohit didn't answer immediately. It was several seconds before he said, "Let's just say the thought crossed my mind."

He was treading carefully. Knowing Puri's closeness to the Deputy Commissioner, he was aware he had to treat the whole matter with kid gloves. That was why he was going to Puri's house himself with a minimum of backup. At this point, with no concrete evidence at his disposal, the last thing he wanted was to give Puri the impression that this was anything more than a polite inquiry.

They had reached Vasant Kunj. Given the lateness of the hour – it was almost midnight – they had encountered very little traffic. Consequently, they were there in less than fifteen minutes.

A police jeep, containing a sub-inspector and three constables, met them outside the Vasant Kunj community center. Mohit got out to speak briefly with the sub-inspector, after which the jeep followed Mohit's car to Puri's residence.

Puri lived in a residential complex located across the street from the Vasant Kunj community center. The complex was surrounded by a fence of corrugated iron. The only way in and out was through a front gate manned by private security guards. The gate was closed at that time of the night and only residents were allowed in. No sooner than Mohit flashed his official credentials, however, the gate swung open for him.

Inside, there were a dozen or so white buildings of three stories each. Puri's flat was situated on the top floor of the building furthest from the gate. Mohit parked his car in the parking lot and, after a brief conversation with the sub-inspector, decided to take one constable up with him. He told the sub-inspector to wait with the other two in the parking lot. If he needed them, he'd call for them on the walkie-talkie. He made no move, however, to prevent Ravi from coming up.

Soon they were standing outside the front door. Mohit pressed the doorbell. Presently the door opened.

A balding, middle-aged man of medium height stood in front of them. He was slim, with a ruddy lean face whose most noticeable feature was a thick graying moustache tapering at both ends of the mouth. He was dressed in a cream-colored kurta-pajama. On his feet, he wore rubber slippers. When he saw Mohit, he stiffened to attention and saluted. Mohit returned the salute.

"I am sorry to intrude at such an hour, S.H.O. Puri," Mohit said.

"O, it's perfectly okay, Sir," Puri said. "I was very much awake. Please come in."

Mohit instructed the constable to wait outside the front door, after which he and Ravi followed Puri to the drawing room, sidestepping past empty cardboard boxes lying in the hall. Puri apologized, saying the flat was still a bit of a mess after last night.

As they entered the drawing room, a young man, dressed in army fatigues, smiled at them from a picture hanging on the opposite wall. The marigold garland round the picture indicated the young man was dead. Ravi guessed this was Puri's son, Abhay.

"His mother and I couldn't stop thinking of him yesterday, Sir," Puri said to Mohit. "He would have been so happy, seeing his little sister getting married."

His voice shook, as he spoke. Mohit patted him on the shoulder. Puri managed a smile and told Mohit and Ravi to make themselves comfortable, while he went and looked in on his wife. He feared she might have been awakened by the doorbell and be wondering who had come calling that late at night.

Ravi and Mohit settled on the sofa. There were bits of colored paper on the floor and a couple of chairs that did not look like they belonged. Other than that, the drawing room had recovered nicely from last night. The furniture was spotless and stood exactly where it should in relation to the room, while the picture frames hung smartly on the walls.

There was a table placed in front of the sofa. On it that day's edition of *The Indian Republic* lay folded. It was the same paper Ravi had seen in Dr. Verma's house in the morning. Above the fold, the story of his father's death occupied the column to the extreme right. Ravi's eyes, however, were drawn to the story next to it, which gave a rundown of road closings and other security precautions being taken for President Musharraf's visit to Delhi. One word in the article had been circled with a blue pen. Ravi leaned forward to get a better look at it. However, he couldn't get past the first part of the word, which was *Raj*, before a hand slid over the paper.

"Excuse me," Puri said.

He picked up the newspaper and deposited it on a table in the corner of the room. Then he asked Mohit and Ravi if they wanted something to drink. After they both shook their heads, he settled in an armchair in front of the sofa.

Mohit started to speak, telling Puri how much he regretted not being able to make it to the wedding last night. He explained it was because his aunt had met with an accident. Puri promptly inquired about her well-being. Mohit said her injuries were not serious, although she had received quite a fright. Puri said at least they could thank god for that, after which he launched into a diatribe against the deteriorating traffic situation in Delhi.

If he was in any way concerned as to why Mohit had come to his house so late at night, he was hiding it well behind the unassuming mask of a junior in the presence of a senior officer. He hadn't even asked about Ravi. He was waiting for Mohit to get to him when he saw fit. Until then, he was quite content to play along with him. Ravi, however, was fast losing patience. It was late and he was tired. The last thing he wanted was to sit and listen to small talk.

Perhaps Mohit sensed Ravi's growing impatience, for, at long last, he came to the point.

"S.H.O. Puri," he said, "this is Ravi Malhotra. He just came from America. He is the son of Ashish Malhotra, the former editor of *The Indian Republic*, who was run over by a car on Thursday evening."

"O, I read about that," Puri said. He turned to Ravi and added, "I am really sorry."

Ravi nodded.

"Have the police caught whoever was responsible?" Puri asked Ravi.

"Not yet," Ravi said.

"The case is registered in your police station," Mohit said to Puri.

"Yes, I thought it would be," Puri said. "According to the

newspaper, Mr. Malhotra was hit not too far from his house in Vasant Vihar. However, I am sorry I don't know too much about the case. I've been on leave all week. Do you know who is investigating it?"

"A.S.I. Kapil investigated it on Thursday evening," Ravi said. "When I called the police station today, however, I learned it had been reassigned to A.S.I. Rawat."

"Good man, Rawat," Puri said. "You are in good hands with him. I'll be sure to speak to him on Monday when I go back to my office. We will try our best to catch the culprit. Let me warn you, though, it is never easy in these hit-and-run cases."

"My father's death was no hit and run."

"Well, that was what the paper said."

"No, my father was murdered."

"Why do you think that?"

Ravi told him what he had learned from Atma Ram. When he was finished, Mohit said, "He believes the people driving the white Ambassador that killed his father were staying in a flat in R.K. Puram, Sector 6."

Puri looked at Ravi who nodded.

"What's the number of this flat?" Puri asked.

"C-16," Ravi said.

He watched Puri's face closely as he spoke. He thought he saw the eyes narrow. That was about it. The surprise, if it existed, was brief and quickly replaced by indignation.

"That's impossible," Puri said. "I know the people staying in C-16. They were right here all day Thursday helping with my daughter's marriage."

"Who are these people, S.H.O. Puri?" Mohit asked.

Puri took a deep breath.

"That flat is assigned to me, Sir," he said. "I plan to sell this flat at the end of the month and move there. After the money I've spent on my daughter's marriage, that's the only way I can stay afloat.

"For the time being, however, I put up some people from my hometown of Gurdaspur who had come to Delhi to help with my daughter's marriage. I would have put them up here. But this is only a two-bedroom flat and I wanted them to be comfortable."

His tone had changed from deferential to pleading. He appeared abashed – a subordinate trying to persuade a superior to look the other way for a transgression. This was Mohit's opportunity to tighten the screws.

"Among the people you put up, S.H.O. Puri, you also had Ganesh Dhawan of the Hindu Tigers," he said. "Was he also in town for your daughter's marriage?"

Puri did not hesitate.

"Yes, Sir," he said. "Ganesh comes from my hometown. My family has long ties with the ashram where he grew up. In fact, the founder of the ashram, who we all call Baba, helped my parents escape from west Pakistan to Gurdaspur during partition. I went to school in that ashram until I was ten. Then we moved away from Gurdaspur and came to Delhi. For many years after that my only contact with that ashram was an annual donation that I sent. It was only after Abhay died that I went back there. It was a terrible time in my life. My son had been my pride and joy, and now he was dead. I didn't think I had anything left to live for. I guess when you feel like that, you always return to the beginning.

"Ganesh and Baba were towers of strength to me in those days. If it hadn't been for them, I doubt if I would have been able to resume my life. Rather than acquit my responsibilities to my wife and daughter, there was a good chance that I would have wasted away.

"And they continue to help me to this day. Baba sent Ganesh to Delhi three weeks ago to help with the marriage preparations. If he hadn't done that, I don't know what I would have done. With Abhay gone, all that running around would have been too much for me at my age."

"But Ganesh Dhawan has a police record," Mohit said. "He is even suspected of murder."

"With due respect, Sir," Puri said, "he has never been convicted or, for that matter, even arrested for murder. And his police record is for his political activities. He is no criminal."

"If you say Dhawan was here to help with your daughter's

marriage, then why was he using an assumed name?" Ravi asked.

"What do you mean?" Puri said.

"In R.K. Puram people thought that Dhawan's name was Vinayak Puri."

"O, that. Well, the flat was allotted to me. As per the rules, only I can live there. So in order to prevent me from getting into trouble, Ganesh might have said his last name was Puri. As for Vinayak – well, that has always been the name that Baba has called Ganesh. You see Baba is from Maharashtra and there Vinayak is another name for Lord Ganesh."

"Where is Dhawan now?" Mohit asked.

"He should be back in Gurdaspur."

Mohit rose to his feet.

"Thank you, S.H.O. Puri," he said. "We will go now and leave you in peace."

Puri stood up as well. He saw the two of them off at the front door.

"I will get on your father's case first thing Monday morning," he promised Ravi.

Ravi and Mohit walked down the stairs in silence. When they reached the bottom of the stairs, Mohit handed Ravi the keys to his car. He said he needed a few minutes with the sub-inspector. Ravi let himself into the car and waited. Presently, Mohit appeared.

"I just sent a message to the control room to alert the police in Gurdaspur about Dhawan," he said. "If Puri was telling the truth, then there is nothing to worry about. Still, I would breathe a lot easier with someone watching Dhawan."

"Do you think he's telling the truth?" Ravi asked.

"I don't know. But right now the only thing I have on him is that he let someone not authorized to stay in government accommodation stay there. That's nothing. It happens all the time. What's more, he provided a perfect alibi for Dhawan and Gokhale when he said they were with him when your father was run over by that car."

Ravi didn't say anything. He was bitterly disappointed. He had believed he was within striking distance of his father's killer. What Puri had said, however, had thrown him right back to square one.

For the rest of the drive, he sat in silence, with his head bowed. Mohit, sensing his disappointment, patted him on the back when they pulled up outside his house.

"Don't worry," he said. "We'll find your father's killer. Come see me in my office on Monday. I will do everything I can."

They said good night. Ravi went inside the house and, after dismissing Hari Singh for the night, collapsed on the drawing-room sofa. He was dead tired, much too tired even to change into his nightclothes and climb into bed.

He took his glasses out of his trousers pockets and placed them on the side table next to the sofa. Then he leaned back and closed his eyes. Maybe, after a few minutes rest, he might just summon the strength to go and change his clothes.

Before he knew it, however, he was fast asleep.

Twenty-seven

Ravi opened his eyes to see the ceiling fan working furiously above him. He was lying on his drawing-room sofa. He was still dressed in the shirt and trousers he had on last night. His shoes and socks, however, lay on the floor and there was a cushion underneath his head.

He sat up and rubbed his eyes. The curtains were drawn on all the windows, as well as the sliding doors. Daylight, however, was beginning to trickle into the room from under the sliding doors. Ravi glanced at his watch. It was ten to seven. He stretched his arms out. He must have fallen asleep when he leaned back on the sofa and closed his eyes. However, he couldn't figure out how he had managed to get his shoes and socks off and placed a cushion under his head.

Sapna entered the room. She was still wearing the jeans and T-shirt she had on last night. The moment he saw her, Ravi recalled his promise to call her once he was done with Puri. He had completely forgotten.

"You are up," she said. "Good morning."

"Good morning."

"We sat up waiting for your call last night. When it didn't come, I tried calling you. There was no answer. Finally, in the morning I decided to come and take a look."

He must have slept right through without hearing the phone ringing. God knew he had been bushed last night. The redness in her eyes, however, indicated she hadn't gotten much sleep herself. He wished he had remembered to call her.

"I'm sorry," he said. "But when I got home last night I was dead. I just sat down on the sofa to rest a few minutes. Before I knew it ..."

He smiled sheepishly and shrugged his shoulders.

"What happened last night?" she asked.

He told her. He ended by saying, "So I guess I'm back to square one."

"Well, at least you got to Puri," she said. "Now he'll make sure you get a proper investigation."

"Yes, he did say he'd get on to it first thing Monday morning. He's been on leave all week. Otherwise I would have asked him why the case was taken away from Kapil after he was sent to investigate it. However, Kapil's supposed to come to work at eight. I think I'll go to the police station and talk to him. I'd better get out there quickly, though. By now the word would have gotten round that I'm home and pretty soon people will be coming to offer their condolences."

"Well, there's no point going there before eight. And right

now it's only seven. Would you like a cup of tea?"

"Yeah, I would. Where's Hari Singh?"

"Probably sitting in his room, wondering what hit him. You see I got here about an hour ago. The guard told me the house was all locked and you weren't up yet. We tried the doorbell. No one answered. I told the guard he simply had to get me in. Otherwise, there would be hell to pay. I guess I scared him, for he promptly woke up Hari Singh. He thought he might have a key. He did not. But I made him stick around while the three of us searched for a door or a window that wasn't bolted. Finally, we did find a window and Hari Singh had to crawl in through it to open the front door. I guess he figured he'd at least get a thank you for his efforts. Instead, I gave him a dressing down for not making sure every window was safely bolted before he left the house last night."

They both laughed.

"You were sleeping so soundly when I came in," she said. "You didn't even make a sound when I made you lie down and put that cushion under your head."

She turned to go to the kitchen. He was left staring after her. He was more than a little surprised by the fact that she had taken the trouble to make him comfortable on the sofa. At the same time, he had to admit that he was pleased. Since coming to India, he had forgotten how good that felt.

He picked up his glasses from the side table next to the sofa. Then he drew the curtains aside. It was cloudy outside.

He could hear Sapna in the kitchen, opening and closing closets in her search for tea leaves. Too late he realized that she was a guest. He toyed with the idea of going to the kitchen to give up on it almost immediately. She might be offended, if he suddenly showed up and started playing host. And insofar as helping her with the tea was concerned, well, he didn't know where the tea leaves were either.

Bahadur came in with the day's newspaper. Ravi put on his glasses and sat down at the dining table to take a look at it. A major chunk of it was devoted to the Pakistani President's visit and the upcoming summit. On the front page itself, there was a box listing Musharraf's program for the day. As he went through it, Ravi learned that soon after arrival Musharraf was supposed to go and lay a wreath at Mahatma Gandhi's memorial at Rajghat.

The word, he had seen circled in the newspaper at Puri's house, had to be Rajghat. But why was Puri interested in the security arrangements for the Pakistani President at Rajghat, especially considering he was out on leave himself?

Sapna arrived with the tea. She looked on with concern, as Ravi added a spoonful of sugar and took his first sip.

"Is it all right?" she asked.

"It's great," he said.

"I didn't know how you liked it. So I made it like I used to for my father, adding a little more milk than usual. I don't like so much myself. But then I'm only half Punjabi."

"Yes, I did wonder about that when I met your grandfather. Sood and Munje –Punjabi and Marathi?"

"Well, my parents fell in love when they were both students at Delhi University. My father came from Jalandhar. At first his parents were dead against the match, as were my mother's parents. In time, however, both families came round. I guess they realized my parents had made up their minds to get married, no matter what."

They sipped their teas. Ravi told her he had seen Rajghat, circled in a newspaper article about security arrangements for Musharraf's visit, at Puri's house last night.

"Why do you think Puri would be interested in something like that," he asked her, "especially considering he's still on leave?"

"I don't know," Sapna said. "Maybe he intends to go somewhere in that area today and was curious if traffic would be disrupted in some way. That's all I can think of."

She paused, then added, "Come to think of it, Musharraf must be one of Puri's least favorite people."

"Why?"

"Well, Musharraf was the architect of the infiltration that resulted in the Kargil war. That was before the military coup in which he overthrew the Pakistani Prime Minister. He was then the army chief. You just told me that Puri's son was killed in that war. If Musharraf hadn't sent those infiltrators in, then the war wouldn't have happened and Puri's son would still be alive. I won't be surprised if Puri sees the entire summit as a sellout. The families of many soldiers who were killed in that war do."

They finished their teas. Sapna rose and said she needed to get back home. The university was closed, since it was Saturday. She planned to spend the day at home. Ravi said he'd call her and promised not to forget this time.

He walked her to the front door. She had come in an autorickshaw. She said she would take one home as well. Ravi, however, would have none of that. He insisted on getting Suresh to drive her home.

They said goodbye in the driveway. He asked her to give his best to her grandfather and, once again, reiterated his promise to call. As he watched the car back out of the gate on to the street, his mind was racing. He figured he could get a quick shower and a change of clothes by the time Suresh returned. By then, it would be eight or thereabouts, time for him to go to the police station and talk to A.S.I. Kapil.

Twenty-eight

The Vasant Vihar police station was about two miles from Ravi's house. Located on Nelson Mandela Road, it was housed in a rectangular four-story building that was painted white and surrounded by a boundary wall. To Ravi, it materialized all of a sudden from behind tall leafy trees, its white visage showing through a veil of green foliage. He was glad he had Suresh to drive him there. On his own, he would probably have missed the place.

Suresh dropped him off in front of the building and made his way to the parking lot. Ravi entered the police station and asked for A.S.I. Kapil at the front desk. The constable, behind the front desk, directed him to an office towards the back. There three desks were set up. Only one, however, had a person manning it. Ravi assumed that was A.S.I. Kapil.

Kapil was dressed in his khaki uniform. He was a young man, possibly in his early thirties. His hair was cut short and parted on the left. He was slim, about five ten, with a narrow, cleanshaven face. He had dark eyes, an aquiline nose and a full mouth.

Ravi walked up to his desk and sat down in the chair facing him. Kapil looked askance.

"A.S.I. Kapil, I am Ravi Malhotra," Ravi said. "I am the son of Ashish Malhotra who was run over by a car on Thursday evening. I believe you were sent to investigate the case."

Kapil was silent. Several seconds passed. Then Kapil's chair scraped back.

"We can't talk here," he said. "Go to Munirka Bazaar. Wait for me there at the Rama Tea Stall. I'll come in fifteen-twenty minutes."

Munirka Bazaar was situated across the street from the police station. Labyrinthene in appearance, it consisted of lines of shops that meandered off the main road into small, dusty alleys. The tea stall, Kapil had mentioned, was well inside the bazaar. With the result, it took Ravi a while to find it.

When he finally did, Ravi sat down at a table to wait. A boy, in his early teens, dressed in dark shorts and a red T-shirt came to take his order. Ravi hesitated. He didn't want anything. However, since he was there, he figured he had to have something. So he told the boy to get him a cup of tea.

The tea stall was a far cry from the upper middle-class environs in which he had grown up. The chairs and tables were all set up under a tarpaulin roof held up by four wooden poles driven into the ground. The tables were bare and, for the most part, well scarred. To relieve the heat, there was a large pedestal fan that made a grating sound as it revolved. Yet even at this hour, with the sun behind the clouds, its impact was minimal. It failed even to disturb the flies that filled the air.

The men, seated at the other tables, were all working-class. They conversed loudly in rough rustic voices, often punctuating what they said with backslaps and guffaws of laughter. Many among them eyed Ravi with interest. They could see he wasn't one of them. When he looked at them, however, they turned away or dropped their eyes.

After a few minutes, Ravi's tea arrived. He was surprised to find it in a glass. He took a sip and grimaced. It was far too milky and sugary. He should have told the boy to bring the milk and sugar separately.

As he continued to sit there, Ravi wished he had worn a lighter shirt with short sleeves. In his haste, he had thrown on the first shirt that came to hand. He rolled up his sleeves and mopped his forehead with his handkerchief, hoping Kapil would come quickly.

When Kapil finally arrived, a little more than thirty minutes had passed since Ravi left him at the police station. At first, Ravi didn't recognize him. Kapil had changed out of his khaki uniform and put on civilian clothes. It was only when he sat down in the chair facing Ravi that Ravi's eyes lit up with recognition.

Kapil ordered tea. Ravi was finding it hard to contain himself. He had been intrigued by Kapil's desire to meet him outside the police station. The fact that Kapil had taken the precaution of changing into civilian clothes only made him that much more curious.

Finally, after a minute that to Ravi seemed an eternity, Kapil said, "Let me start right at the beginning.

"On Thursday I was working the four-to-twelve shift. When the phone call came about your father's accident, it was my turn on the rotation. At the time, I didn't know your father was involved. All I knew was that there had been an accident. I learned about your father only at the hospital.

"Your father was already dead by the time I reached the hospital. So I went on to the site of the accident. There I spoke to the fruit seller Atma Ram. After speaking to him, I was convinced it wasn't an accident, but a premeditated murder. When I went to your house, your servant told me you were expected from America later that night. I took down your phone number, thinking I'd get in touch with you in the morning.

"However, when I returned to the police station, I found a message from the S.H.O. waiting for me. He wanted to see me in his office right away."

"What?" Ravi said.

He stared at Kapil.

"You're telling me the S.H.O. was in his office on Thursday night?" he said. "The very night his daughter was getting married?"

"Yes," Kapil said. "I too was surprised. He hadn't been in all week and the last day I expected him to come in was Thursday and that, too, at night."

So Puri had lied. If he had spoken to Kapil that night, he had to have known that his father had been murdered on Thursday itself.

Kapil continued.

"The S.H.O. wasn't alone," he said. "There was another man in the office with him – a much older man who he said was a plainclothes policeman."

"A much older man," Ravi said. "How much older?"

"Well, he had to be more than sixty-five, perhaps even over seventy. I was rather taken aback to learn that he was a plainclothes policeman. I know quite a few of them and, though the man looked fit, he was much too old."

Could that man be Aditya Gokhale? He certainly fitted into the age bracket that Kapil had mentioned.

"What was this man's name?" Ravi asked.

"The S.H.O. introduced him as Khanna," Kapil said. "He nodded to me when we were introduced. However, I don't remember him saying one word. The whole time I was there, he simply sat in his chair and watched me."

"What did the S.H.O. want with you?"

"He wanted to know what I had found out in your father's case. He said that he had got a message from headquarters that the case I was investigating involved the well-known journalist Ashish Malhotra. Now I was well and truly foxed. I hadn't known the victim until I reached the hospital. From there I had gone straight to the site of the accident. I hadn't reported anything to anyone, least of all to headquarters. I was going to do all that when I returned to the police station. The news hadn't hit the media yet. So how did the S.H.O. know the identity of the victim? He certainly couldn't have got it from headquarters."

He had got it from Gokhale and Dhawan. They had known, because they had killed his father, either individually or collectively. Puri was at the police station that night to forestall any investigation that might implicate them.

What Kapil said next simply confirmed what Ravi was thinking.

"I told the S.H.O. everything I had found out," he said. "I concluded by saying I thought that your father had been murdered. There was pindrop silence when I finished. Then the S.H.O. and the man he said was a plainclothes policeman exchanged a look, after which the S.H.O. said he was taking me off the case. I couldn't believe my ears. I asked him why. He said since such an eminent man was involved, he wanted someone with more experience on the case. I almost fell out of my chair. I am one of the most experienced A.S.I.s at the station.

"I tried to persuade him to let me stay on the case. But he

was adamant. Finally, I had to give in. After all, he did outrank me. I asked him who he had in mind as my replacement so that I could give my report to him. I didn't think there was much of an issue there. If he wanted someone more experienced than me, then the choice was between two men – Kumar and Mathur. Since Kumar, like me, had the four-to-twelve shift, he was the automatic choice. The S.H.O., however, said he'd think about it and get back to me. Then he told me to go.

"Later, I found that he had given the case to Rawat. Rawat is four years my junior. So all that talk about getting a more experienced man was crap. In addition, to add insult to injury, he moved me to the eight-to-four shift with immediate effect."

Kapil's voice was raised when he finished. Clearly, he was still angry with the way he had been treated.

"Why do you think he put this Rawat on the case?" Ravi asked him.

"Because Rawat is his lapdog. He does exactly what Puri tells him to do. And it's clear that Puri has a personal interest in the case, one strong enough for him to leave his daughter on her wedding night and come to the office."

He leaned forward.

"Mr. Malhotra," he said, "I have told you everything I know. Now I need you to tell me what you know. There is something terribly wrong going on here."

Ravi was silent, wondering whether he should tell him. After a short pause, he decided to go ahead. Kapil, after all, had been candid with him. Furthermore, it was obvious that Kapil wanted to help and he needed all the help he could get to bring his father's killers to book.

He told Kapil that his father had stumbled upon Ganesh Dhawan and an old man, he was certain was Aditya Gokhale, in a flat assigned to Puri in R.K. Puram. Kapil's eyebrows rose at the mention of Dhawan and the Hindu Tigers. Ravi said he was convinced that his father had been killed by Dhawan and Gokhale. They obviously had something planned for this weekend's summit and the last thing they wanted was a journalist snooping about. He had come to that conclusion yesterday itself. However, when Mohit and he went to Puri's house last night, Puri threw a spanner in the works by providing an alibi for Dhawan and Gokhale, saying they were in town for his daughter's wedding. Now, however, after talking to Kapil, Ravi could see that was a lie. And since Puri was clearly covering up for Dhawan and Gokhale, he had to be part of whatever they had in mind.

"I am sure the man Puri introduced as Khanna was really Aditya Gokhale," he said. "He fits the description."

Kapil didn't speak. He appeared deep in thought, as he sat staring into the distance. Finally, he said, "When I was leaving Puri's office on Thursday night, my notes fell out of the file I had brought with me just as I opened the door. As I bent down to pick them up, Puri's phone rang. Puri's desk is placed in such a way that the phone is to his right and the door to his left. So he couldn't see me when he picked up the phone. I guess he thought I had already left, for he spoke briefly into the receiver and then shut up. Possibly the other man indicated to him that I was still there. Then he did not speak until I closed the door behind me.

"However, I did hear him say, 'Yes, Dharam, it's all taken care of. He's with me now. He should be at Rajghat on Saturday morning.'"

Rajghat. That word again.

"By *he* the S.H.O. must have meant the man with him," Kapil continued. "And General Musharraf is supposed to go to Rajghat to lay a wreath at Mahatma Gandhi's memorial this morning. So if ..."

"Who's Dharam?" Ravi interrupted.

"The only other time I have heard the S.H.O. use that name was one time when he was talking to the Deputy Commissioner of Security," Kapil said. "His first name is Dharamvir – Dharamvir Sethi."

Ravi stared at him, his eyes widening as the realization hit him.

Twenty-nine

Kapil leaned across the table and shook Ravi by the shoulder. Ravi blinked.

"What happened?" Kapil asked. "You've been sitting there as if you're in some kind of trance. You don't answer. You don't say anything. What's going on?"

He was looking concerned. Ravi took a deep breath.

"They are going to kill Musharraf," he said.

"What?" Kapil said.

"When you told me about that phone call, everything fell into place. Just think about it. By assassinating Musharraf, Dhawan and Gokhale accomplish two things. First they kill the summit even before it begins. Then, with the assassination taking place on Indian soil, they raise the question of the complicity of the Indian government. Muslim radicals in Pakistan, who are as opposed to peace as Hindu radicals in India, would be sure to hammer that point home. In any event, the net result would be that any chance of peace between the two nations would be snuffed out, leaving them at loggerheads with the possibility of an all-out war lurking in the background.

That's exactly what Dhawan and Gokhale want. In their eyes, such a situation allows them to inch that much closer to their goal of unifying India, which they believe can only be done by defeating Pakistan on the battlefield."

Kapil was silent. Then, after a short pause, he said, "How is Puri involved in all this?"

"His motivation is entirely different," Ravi said, "as is Sethi's. They want Musharraf dead to get even for the loss of their sons.

"They are both crucial to the success of the plan, Sethi more so than Puri as he is in charge of security. Without him, an assassin would find it hard to get close to Musharraf. Puri is simply the facilitator. He's the one who brought Dhawan and Gokhale together with Sethi.

"Dhawan and Gokhale came to Delhi a few weeks ago, possibly to acquaint themselves with the place as well as chalk out a strategy for the assassination. They holed up in a government flat assigned to Puri. The setup was perfect. They needed anonymity to carry out their designs, especially since Dhawan was a marked man. Therefore, a government flat, allotted to a police officer, made for an ideal nesting place.

"Then the unforeseen happened. They ran into my father.

"Suddenly they were confronted with the danger of losing their anonymity in the worst possible way. That wasn't a risk they were willing to accept, not when they had come so close to accomplishing their goal.

"So they decided to kill my father.

"Luckily for them, he lived in Vasant Vihar, where Puri was the S.H.O. Therefore, as long as they killed him in Vasant Vihar, they stood every chance of getting away, since they had Puri to cover for them. The best way to do it was to make it look like an accident. That gave Puri the option to close the book on any murder investigation and simply dismiss it as a hit-and-run case.

"But that also meant they could only do it when my father left the house. And they had no idea when that was going to happen. If he had been working, at least they could have assumed that he would leave for his office in the morning. But now he was retired; he could come and go as he pleased.

"So they had no alternative, but to wait their chance. Puri, however, couldn't do that. His daughter was getting married the same day and with hectic last-minute preparations underway, the last thing he could do was sit and wait in his office. As a result, by the time he got the word and rushed to his office, you had already left to investigate the case.

"Then Dhawan and Gokhale queered things up by being overcautious. By concealing the license plates of their car, they raised a question mark as to whether it was really an accident in the mind of the onlooker.

"Even then, Puri could have handled things. By replacing you with his stooge, he could turn the investigation whichever way he wanted. However, I arrived from America and, almost immediately, started asking questions. Mohit and I showed up at Puri's residence, armed with the knowledge that Dhawan and Gokhale had stayed in a flat assigned to him. Puri was forced to take cover behind his daughter's marriage and tell us that Dhawan and Gokhale were old friends who had come into town to help with the marriage preparations. He had put them up in the flat assigned to him in R.K. Puram, because his flat in Vasant Kunj was much too small. Such an explanation allowed Puri to establish an alibi for Dhawan and Gokhale, while explaining away their presence in Delhi.

"Furthermore, he told Mohit and me that Dhawan had returned to Gurdaspur the day after the marriage. He didn't say anything about Gokhale, though. In the case of Dhawan, he was probably telling the truth. Gokhale would have needed the younger man in Delhi to do the running about, while he was figuring out how to kill Musharraf. But he is quite capable of killing him on his own, especially considering he has Sethi's help. Furthermore, with Gokhale, rather than Dhawan pulling the trigger, there is a far greater chance of success. Dhawan has a police record. He's also a young man. The entire police force would be on the lookout for someone like him. Removing him from the scene not only lulls the authorities into a false sense of security, it also makes sure that he is far too removed from the assassination to be swept up in its aftermath.

"Gokhale is going to do it. With the help of Sethi he will get into Rajghat, possibly as a plainclothes policeman. There he will kill Musharraf and, in all probability, die himself. That way all the secrets will go with him, leaving the others free to get on with their lives. Soon after the summit was announced, Gokhale stepped down as head of his ashram. He is nearing the end of his life. Given his age, he might never get another chance to do something glorious for the Cause. From all standpoints, the time is right for him to make the ultimate sacrifice."

He was finished. Kapil, who had listened intently to the entire monologue, looked at his watch.

'It's nine fifteen," he said. "Musharraf is due at Rajghat a little after ten."

He sprang to his feet, throwing some rupee notes on the table. Ravi rose as well.

"Where are you going?" he asked.

"Rajghat," Kapil answered. "I know A.C.P. Mohit Prasad is there this morning. The only way to prevent the assassination is to get to him as quickly as possible. Although he is junior to the Deputy Commissioner, he is still a high-ranking officer. He can employ the resources necessary to stop the assassination. He may even be able to stop Musharraf from coming to Rajghat. Then, since he knows the background of your father's murder, he won't take much convincing. The others will ask a million questions. With the result, we will lose valuable time."

"Rajghat isn't exactly next door," Ravi said. "Surely there is a faster way to get in touch with Mohit than going there. What about the phone or the police radio?"

Kapil laughed.

"Seems you have no idea how hierarchical the police is," he said. "Well, I guess you can be excused since you don't live in India.

"You are a civilian, while I am just a lowly A.S.I. Before we can get through to the A.C.P., we will first have to convince a host of underlings as to why we need to speak to him so urgently. To make them believe that the Deputy Commissioner is part of the assassination plot will take some doing. We simply don't have the time for that. Furthermore, if I saw Aditya Gokhale as recently as Thursday night, I should be at Rajghat to help identify him."

He broke into a run. Ravi followed.

"How do we get there?" Ravi asked.

"We'll take a jeep from the police station," Kapil said. "We can then use the siren to get through the traffic and we won't have to stop at traffic lights. We can also use roads that are closed to the public. Come on."

The police jeep skidded to a stop by the kerb outside the sprawling Rajghat complex. Even though they had been in a police vehicle, it had still taken them almost thirty minutes to reach Rajghat. Ravi and Kapil jumped out to run to the entrance, which was decked in marigold flowers. A constable blocked their path. Kapil showed him his police ID and said he needed to see Mohit immediately. The constable said he had orders not to let anyone through without security clearance. His voice, however, lacked firmness. He was clearly intimidated by the fact that Kapil outranked him. It didn't take Kapil long to convince him that his best interests lay in letting them pass.

No sooner than they were inside, however, they ran into another obstacle. A well-built man, dressed in a dark suit, stood in front of them. The walkie-talkie in his hand indicated he was either with the police or the special security forces. Ravi grimaced. He didn't think they were going to get through this roadblock so easily.

Then he spotted Mohit coming towards them at a run. He was wearing a dark suit. In his right hand, he carried a walkie-talkie. Ravi called out to him. Mohit, if he heard him, didn't place him at first. As he came closer, however, his eyes widened and he stopped dead on the walkway.

"What are *you* doing here?" he asked Ravi.

"You know these people?" the other man in the suit asked him.

Mohit glanced at Kapil who promptly saluted.

"Yes, yes, they are all right," he said.

He turned to the other man.

"We just got word that Musharraf's convoy is running early," he said. "He should be here in the next ten minutes. You'd better go alert your men."

The other man hurried off, barking orders in his walkie-talkie.

"What the hell are you doing here?" Mohit asked Ravi.

"They are out to kill Musharraf," Ravi said.

"What?'

"Yes, and they are going to do it right here."

"But early this morning the police in Gurdaspur confirmed that Dhawan is indeed in Gurdaspur. What's more, they have a twenty-four-hour watch on him."

"It's not Dhawan, it's Gokhale. A.S.I. Kapil here heard them talking about it."

"Heard *who* talking about it?"

"D.C.P. Sethi and S.H.O. Puri, Sir," Kapil said. "I was leaving S.H.O. Puri's office on Thursday night when D.C.P. Sethi called. The S.H.O. must have thought I was already gone. Otherwise, I am sure he wouldn't have spoken so freely. He shut up the moment he realized I was still there."

"Aditya Gokhale was also in the room with him at the time," Ravi said. "Puri introduced him as Khanna and told Kapil that he was a plainclothes policeman. Both Sethi and Puri want Musharraf dead to get even for the loss of their sons; Musharraf was the Pakistani army chief during the Kargil war. So they are helping Dhawan and Gokhale. Dhawan and Gokhale were scared my father would get suspicious and jeopardize the entire plan. So they killed him. Then Puri tried to protect them by transferring the case from Kapil to one of his stooges."

Kapil nodded.

"Sir, Gokhale is supposed to be at Rajghat this morning," he said. "We believe he is posing as a plainclothes policeman with D.C.P. Sethi's help."

Mohit was looking blankly from one man to the other. Clearly, things were going much too fast for him. Just moments ago, secure in the knowledge that Dhawan was in Gurdaspur and under police watch, he had been certain the danger was past. Now he was being told that an attempt on the Pakistani President's life could be moments away. He needed time to make the adjustment.

"Sir, you must radio the convoy and stop them from coming here," Kapil said.

All around them, the place had exploded into activity. Unmindful of the light drizzle that had sprung up, an assortment of people was hurrying into position. A welcoming committee was gathering outside the entrance. Security men were running about, making sure all arrangements were in place. Mediapersons were making last-minute preparations . . . Amid this flurry of activity, Mohit finally found his voice.

"I can't stop the convoy," he said. "Only Sethi can."

The bewildered look was gone from his face. The adjustment had been made.

"What does Gokhale look like?" he asked Kapil.

"He's cleanshaven, with a shock of white hair," Kapil said. "For a man his age he is in pretty good shape – slim, tall, broad-shouldered."

"We can't search the whole place in the time we have. It's much too big. However, Musharraf is not going everywhere. So if Gokhale plans to kill him, he'll probably be waiting at a spot that Musharraf is expected to visit. That includes the Rajghat office where he will sign the visitors' book, the shrine itself where he will pay his respects to Gandhi, the ..."

He continued to speak. Ravi, however, was no longer listening. Something Mohit had just said had triggered a memory.

"Listen," he said, raising a hand.

Mohit grew silent.

"If we know anything about Gokhale it is that he is inspired by Godse," Ravi said. "He kept the book Godse presented him all these years. Then this assassination is supposed to take place at Rajghat – the memorial to the man Godse killed."

"Go on," Mohit said.

"Well, if I remember correctly, just before Godse shot Gandhi, he actually paid his respects to him by folding his hands. As a hardcore Hindu nationalist he may have hated Gandhi's politics, but he respected him as a man of god."

Mohit stared at him. Then he said, "Come on."

The three of them began to run in the direction of the shrine.

Up the walkway they went to enter the foreclosure, where visitors were supposed to take off their shoes before entering the shrine to pay their respects. The man, manning the counter where you were supposed to deposit your shoes, shouted, "You can't go in there like this." He moved as if to block their path. The constable on guard, however, held him back.

"Is there anyone inside?" Mohit asked the constable.

"There is a plainclothes policeman who just went in," the constable answered.

"Is he an old man, tall, with white hair?"

"Yes."

"Come with us."

The constable followed the three of them through the foreclosure, after which they entered the garden that surrounded the shrine. The shrine was located on a concrete island in the center of the garden. It consisted of a black granite slab, which received floral offerings, near which the eternal flame glowed in a glass case. At the moment, it was deserted, except for the solitary figure of a tall, white-haired man, dressed in brown trousers and a short-sleeved white shirt. He stood barefoot, with his back to them. His head was bowed; he was meditating.

That had to be Gokhale.

Mohit sprinted towards him with his pistol out. Gokhale apparently heard him coming, for his head jerked up and he began to turn around. But he was too late. The pistol butt caught him on the head and he folded to the ground.

No sooner than he fell, strains of Kabir's couplet 'Ram Rahim ek hain' sounded over the public address system.

Musharraf had arrived.

Thirty

It was Mohit's idea to move Gokhale as soon as possible. He figured that Musharraf would soon be making his way to the shrine to pay his respects. The last thing he wanted was for him to be greeted by the sight of an unconscious Gokhale.

Ravi agreed that Gokhale needed to be removed. However, he was surprised when Mohit did not call for a stretcher. There was an ambulance on standby right outside Rajghat and one word from Mohit on his walkie-talkie could have stretcher bearers on the scene in a matter of minutes. Then Gokhale was bleeding; a bruise had formed on the spot where Mohit had hit him with his gun. He could do with some first-aid.

Mohit, however, decided they would carry Gokhale out of Rajghat. He watched, as Kapil frisked him to remove a revolver from his trousers pockets. Then, while Kapil bandaged his head with a handkerchief, Mohit called his driver on his cellphone and instructed him to meet him with the jeep at the back of Rajghat.

Kapil and the constable lifted Gokhale. As they started making their way to the back of Rajghat, Mohit explained what he was doing to Ravi. He said it was the only way to get Gokhale out of Rajghat without Sethi's knowledge. For if Sethi got to know that Gokhale was in Mohit's custody, he'd surely try to get him released. Given his rank, he might even succeed. Therefore, what they needed to do was to get Gokhale out of Rajghat with the minimum of fuss and the maximum of haste.

Ravi listened to what Mohit had to say. However, he was not convinced. Agreed, Sethi was the superior officer. But Mohit had caught Gokhale red-handed, masquerading as a plainclothes policeman in a restricted area. Furthermore, Gokhale had been armed. Surely, that was enough for Mohit to hold him, in spite of Sethi.

Kapil and the constable, however, appeared to have no problems with what Mohit was doing. Therefore, Ravi, finding himself in a minority, kept his misgivings to himself.

Their way out led them through the foreclosure. The man, at the counter to deposit shoes, gazed pointedly at the bloodstained handkerchief on Gokhale's head. Mohit told him that Gokhale had collapsed from the heat and hurt himself when his head hit the ground. The man glanced at the cloudy sky and the falling drizzle. But he said nothing.

With everyone's attention focused on Musharraf at the other end of Rajghat, they were able to make their way to the back gate without any trouble. The only people they encountered were security men standing guard at various points. The sight of the four of them with an unconscious man, wearing a bloody makeshift bandage on his head, drew plenty of stares. But no one said anything. The presence of Mohit guaranteed that. The security men knew who he was and the last thing any one of them wanted was to take issue with him. In fact, Mohit had to refuse a few who were keen to help carry the unconscious man.

Finally, they reached the back gate, where Mohit's driver was waiting with the jeep. The jeep was a Delhi Police vehicle – a Maruti Gypsy painted white, with a roof and the Delhi Police slogan WITH YOU FOR YOU ALWAYS inscribed in red in English and Hindi all over the outside. Kapil had to fold Gokhale's legs to make him fit, lying down, in the back of the jeep. Then he climbed in with him. Ravi squeezed in as well. Mohit, however, lingered to have a word with the constable. Ravi couldn't hear what he said to him. However, he could see the constable nodding. When Mohit was finished, the constable saluted him. Then he hurried off to return to his post. Mohit climbed into the front of the jeep to sit beside the driver. He told the driver to take them to Tihar jail.

After they were on their way, Mohit used the cellphone again to call the jail superintendent, telling him he was on his way with a prisoner who was hurt. He said he'd supply the details when he arrived. However, he stressed the importance of the prisoner repeatedly, asking the superintendent not to tell anyone that he was coming, until he actually got there.

Ravi, seated in the back of the jeep, could hear Mohit

through the glass partition. With each passing moment, he was getting more than a little bemused by the way Mohit was handling things. Not only had he smuggled Gokhale out of Rajghat, he appeared intent on smuggling him into Tihar jail as well. He couldn't figure out why Mohit was taking Gokhale to Tihar in the first place. The jail had to be at least forty minutes away.

He wondered whether he should ask Kapil, then promptly gave up on the idea. He had seen enough of how the police worked to figure out the last thing Kapil would do was speculate on a superior officer's intentions, especially with that officer sitting well within earshot.

A murmur from Gokhale cut into his thoughts. Ravi looked at him. Was he regaining consciousness? A little later, however, he looked away. The murmur had been a false alarm. Gokhale was still very much out.

They made fast progress through the traffic and were at Tihar in less than forty minutes. When they entered the jail compound, Gokhale was still unconscious. There a couple of stretcher bearers were waiting for him. They whisked him away on a stretcher. Mohit and Kapil went with them, accompanied by the jail superintendent. Ravi was asked to wait at the reception. Only police personnel were allowed in the area where Gokhale was taken.

Ravi sat down to wait. The easy familiarity with which Mohit and the jail superintendent had greeted each other confirmed his suspicion that the two men were good friends. Whether it was the jail superintendent or his driver, Mohit was taking great pains to expose Gokhale only to people that were close to him in the police force. He had even used his cellphone, rather than the walkie-talkie or the police radio, to get in touch with them. Was that also because of Sethi?

Fifteen minutes dragged past. Finding it hard to contain himself, Ravi rose and started to pace. Another five minutes passed. Still there was no sign of anybody. Finally, Ravi could take it no longer. He walked up to the receptionist and demanded to know what was going on. The receptionist pleaded ignorance and asked Ravi to be patient. Ravi, however, looked him straight in the eye and told him if he didn't find out what was happening in the next few minutes, he was going to barge into the superintendent's office himself. Seeing that Ravi was in dead earnest, the receptionist said he'd get on the job immediately and requested him to sit down.

For the next minute or so, the receptionist was on the phone. As a result, soon Mohit appeared.

"What's the matter?" he asked Ravi.

"I want to know what's going on with Gokhale," Ravi said.

"Well, he's conscious now. However, the prison doctor is still examining the bruise to his head."

"When can I see him?"

"Not anytime soon. Even if the doctor says he doesn't have to be hospitalized, we have to complete certain formalities before he can see anyone. In fact, I don't think you'll be able to see him today. It's best if you go back home. The moment he's ready to see you, I promise I'll give you a call."

"I'm not going anywhere without seeing him. I'm prepared to wait here for days if necessary."

Mohit gritted his teeth. Ravi could see he was angry. But he was determined to get to Gokhale, no matter what.

"If it wasn't for me, you wouldn't have Gokhale right now," he told Mohit. "In fact, far from having him, you'd be busy explaining away an assassination. All I am asking in return is a few minutes alone with Gokhale. Can't you even give me that?"

Mohit took a deep breath.

'Stay right here," he said. "I'll see what I can do."

Ravi sat down. It was almost twenty minutes before Mohit reappeared.

"Come on," he said to Ravi.

Ravi rose. He followed Mohit down a long corridor to a room in the corner of the building. A police guard was standing outside the door.

"I'll stay right here," Mohit said, pausing outside the door. "You've got fifteen minutes."

Ravi nodded and opened the door to go in. The room inside was small, with no windows. A ceiling fan that hung from a low roof over the center of the room provided the only relief from the heat. Directly below the ceiling fan was a table, across which two straight-backed chairs faced each other. The floor was bare, the walls painted white. The room was lit by a tube light, attached to the wall to the right of the door.

Gokhale was seated in the chair that faced the door. He was still dressed in the clothes he had been wearing at Rajghat. His shirt was stained with dried blood, while a bandage covered most of his head. Other than that, he showed no ill effects of the blow. The eyes that greeted Ravi were as alert as any.

Ravi closed the door behind him. He hesitated, briefly, then stepped over to sit in the chair across the table from Gokhale. He could feel Gokhale's eyes on him. They hadn't left him for an instant since he entered the room. Now they traveled over his face, examining each detail.

"You must be Ranbir's son," he said.

His voice was heavy, like that of an old-time theatre actor. Ravi nodded.

"You look just like him," Gokhale continued. "The same hair, eyes, nose … It's uncanny."

He shook his head.

"Your father told me about you," he said. "He said you were coming from America."

"Did he tell you why I was coming?" Ravi asked.

Gokhale didn't answer.

"I was coming to take him back with me," Ravi said. "My

father didn't have more than a year left to live. He dearly wanted to spend his last days with me. And I wanted the same, just as badly. By killing him, you robbed both of us of that chance."

Gokhale was quiet, looking down. After a brief pause, he said, "That couldn't be helped."

"Why? So that you could kill another man?"

"What do you think I am? Some sort of common murderer? Do you think I kill people because I like it? You don't know how much your father's death pained me. He was my boyhood friend. You can't imagine how happy I was to see him after more than fifty years."

He sighed.

"You won't understand," he said. "Someone like you, raised in the lap of luxury ... What do *you* know about giving yourself to a Cause, to something bigger than any friend or relative, any human being? Your father didn't either. Otherwise, he would never have drifted away from the Cause as he did.

"When you give yourself to a Cause, it becomes as much a part of you as your flesh and blood. It's the air you breathe, the food you eat, the water you drink ... It's with you every waking moment, and you are prepared to do anything for it – to give your life if necessary, as also take another life.

"When your father came to see me, it soon became apparent that he was going to be trouble. The way he was looking at

Vinayak, the questions he was asking him ... If there were a way, I would have taken him into confidence. But I couldn't do that. There was no way he would have understood what we were trying to do. He had drifted much too far from the Cause.

"Still, it wasn't easy for me. Even when I was behind the wheel of the car and he was there right in front of me, I paused to think if there was a way that I could spare him. But there wasn't. Letting him live meant that I could fail. And I had come much too far to take that chance."

"But fail you did," Ravi said. "Musharraf is still alive and you are here in jail."

Gokhale sighed.

"That would never have happened if it were not for Vinayak and Puri," he said. "Vinayak came to Delhi a few days before I did. I had to stay behind to tie up a few things at the ashram. Without telling me, he hired the Nepali boy as a cook. Agreed, he couldn't cook himself. But given what we were doing, the last thing we needed was a stranger in the house. If it hadn't been for that, your father would never have found me. Even after he did, I would have handled things if were not for Puri. He got cold feet the moment he learned your father had stumbled on to Vinayak and me. He wanted to call the whole thing off. The D.C.P. and I had to lean on him to keep him in line. Even then, he didn't go to his office as he was supposed to, on Thursday. I only found out he wasn't there after your father was dead. Immediately, I called the D.C.P. The two of us had to twist his arm to make him go. Seeing how reluctant he was, I decided to go along with him. I was afraid he'd lose his nerve if he went on his own. If he had been in his office as we had agreed, your father's case would never have gone to A.S.I. Kapil.

"Anyway, my conscience is clear. I did the best I could, and I'd do it again without a moment's thought."

His voice was steady, his eyes level. Ravi shook his head.

"I wanted to see for myself what kind of man you are," he said. "Now that I have, I don't think I will have any problems when the judge passes the death sentence on you. In fact, I might even cheer."

Gokhale threw back his head and laughed. He laughed so hard that he almost fell out of his chair. Ravi stared at him. This was the last thing he could have expected.

"God, you are so naive," Gokhale said, as he simmered down. "My dear boy, there's going to be no trial. In fact, the world is not even going to know what I did. For if any of that gets out, too many people are going to look very foolish. To think someone like me could come so close to assassinating a foreign dignitary! Then just imagine the scope of the scandal. Two police officers, one of them a D.C.P., involved in a plot to assassinate a visiting head of state! Who wants that? Not the politicians, not the bureaucrats, and certainly not the police.

"Why do you think your A.C.P. hit me on the head and

smuggled me here in his jeep? Why didn't he arrest me, as he was supposed to, and march me out of there in full view of everyone? Because he knew that would draw attention. The media would get involved and the whole story would come out. To make sure that wouldn't happen, he didn't even call for an ambulance.

"The last thing everyone wants is a public trial. To avoid that, they will get rid of me as soon as possible and then hush everything up. Not that it makes any difference to me. I knew I was a dead man the moment I made up my mind to kill Musharraf. I just wish I was taking him with me."

The door to the room swung open. Mohit stood in the doorway.

"Come on, Ravi," he said. "Time's up."

Ravi remained where he was. Mohit came in and shook him by the shoulder.

"Come on," he said.

Slowly, Ravi rose to his feet and walked to the door. Before going outside, however, he turned around to look at Gokhale. Gokhale smiled and raised a hand in farewell.

There were two policemen standing outside, presumably to take Gokhale away. Mohit had a word with them. Then Ravi and he began walking down the corridor in the direction of the reception. They had gone about ten paces when Ravi asked, "What happens now?"

"Well, I have spoken to my superiors," Mohit said. "They should be coming soon. Once they are here, we'll discuss what kind of charges we can frame against him."

"What about Puri and Sethi?"

"Them, too?"

"Have they been arrested?"

"I don't know. However, I have passed the word on to my superiors.'

Ravi stopped walking. Mohit halted as well, giving Ravi a quizzical look.

"What's the matter?" he asked.

"Will you stop bullshitting me?" Ravi said.

"What do you mean?" Mohit said.

"The whole morning I was trying to figure out why you were doing what you were doing. Now it all finally makes sense. You are not going to charge Gokhale. You will simply make him disappear. The police and the security forces can't just admit to the world that someone could come so close to killing a foreign dignitary. And then there's the whole issue of Puri and Sethi. You all can't afford such a scandal, can you? Why, even now your superiors must be talking to them about early retirement; some sudden desire to spend more time with the family, with full pension and other benefits of course. That way everyone's happy. Puri and Sethi don't go to jail and the police get rid of the black sheep without the whiff of a public scandal. That leaves Dhawan, Kapil, the constable at Rajghat, and me. Well, Kapil and the constable are the easiest. After all, they are policemen. They are bound to be concerned about the image of the police. Then I am sure a promotion with a hike in salary is in the offing. And Dhawan? Well, he expected Gokhale to die, anyway. Furthermore, he has his own neck to save. Even though he wasn't at Rajghat today, he could still go to jail for several years for helping Gokhale. So he can be counted on to keep his mouth shut. That leaves me. Well, tell me, how do you plan to buy me off? And what happens if I don't play ball? Do I also disappear like Gokhale?"

Mohit's face had remained impassive right through the long tirade. Now he took a deep breath.

"As far as we are concerned, your father died in a hit-and-run accident," he said. "That's what Kapil is recording in his report. Since no one saw the license plate number of the car, we don't know who it was – case closed. As for the plot to kill Musharraf, you have no one to corroborate your story, no physical evidence, nothing whatsoever. No one will believe a word that you say. All you will end up doing is making a laughing stock out of yourself."

He placed his hand on Ravi's shoulder.

"I am telling you this as a friend, Ravi," he said. "Go home, get some rest and try to put all this behind you. As for your father's killer, let us take care of him for you."

Ravi stared at him. Then he shrugged his hand off and walked away, leaving Mohit gazing after him.

Epilogue

As it was a Saturday night, there were far fewer private vehicles on the Delhi-Chandigarh highway than was usually the case. Therefore, the minivan, with the Punjab license plates, represented something of an anomaly as it made its way among the many trucks and buses.

There were two men in the minivan. They were both young, in their late twenties or early thirties. They were both dressed in a shirt and trousers. They had been driving for almost seven hours, having started from Gurdaspur round six that evening. Other than stopping once for gas and a quick bite to eat, they had driven nonstop.

For most of the drive, they had been silent. One time the man, behind the wheel, turned on the radio to listen to the news. No sooner than the announcer finished with the headlines, however, he turned the radio off. His sombre face indicated he had far too much on his mind. The same was true of his companion.

About fifty miles from Delhi, the minivan swung off the highway to bump along on a dirt track. After ten minutes or so, it entered a field where a matador stood waiting with its lights on.

The two men got out of the minivan, squinting as flashlights hit them in the face.

"Get your hands up," the man, holding one of the flashlights, said.

The two men raised their hands. They were frisked. After they were dubbed clean, the man, who had told them to raise their hands, walked up to them. It was Mohit, dressed in a shirt and trousers.

"Ganesh Dhawan?" he said.

"Yes," the man, who had been driving the minivan, answered.

Mohit shone the flashlight into his face. After he was satisfied, he turned and said, "Bring the body."

Two policemen, dressed in civilian clothes, picked up the body from the back of the matador. It was wrapped in a white sheet. They carried it to where Mohit stood. Dhawan stepped forward and pulled the sheet back from over the head to close his eyes momentarily as he recognized Gokhale. Then he put the sheet back over the head.

"We'll take him from here," he said.

He nodded to his companion. The two men took over from the two policemen. One of the policemen made as if to help them. Dhawan, however, held up his hand.

Mohit waited, until Dhawan and his companion had placed the body in the back of the minivan. Then he said to Dhawan, "Remember if any of this ever gets out, you will have hell to pay."

Dhawan nodded. Mohit and the other policemen drove off in the matador, leaving Dhawan and his companion standing next to the minivan.

Dhawan's companion had tears in his eyes. Dhawan placed his arm round his shoulders.

"Don't worry," he said. "For every one of us they kill, there are at least two more born every day. One day there will be so many that no one will be able to stop us."

It was a small group that gathered at the cremation ground on Sunday morning. Ravi figured that was how his father would have wanted it. Despite the public nature of his profession, his father was an intensely private man. With the result, while hc knew a lot of people, he was close to very few. Those were the ones he would want at his funeral.

They were, for the most part, old cronies from *The Indian Republic*. There were also men like Dr. Verma, an acquaintance from his club who had evolved into a personal friend. A close-knit group, they went back several decades with his father, some as far back as half a century. With the result, they looked quizzically at Sapna and Munje. They were clearly surprised to see a couple of strangers in their midst.

After the cremation, Ravi went back home and, as per custom, cleansed himself with a bath. Then he donned a shirt and a pair of trousers, putting aside the white kurta-pajama he had worn to the funeral. By the time he was dressed, Hari Singh was waiting with a late breakfast. Ravi wasn't hungry. However, since he hadn't eaten all morning, he decided to have some.

After breakfast, he let Hari Singh go to make his own food and wandered about the house. The last two days, he had been preoccupied with his father's murder and then the funeral. It seemed, all that time, an entire cast of memories had waited their turn in the shadows and were now stepping out into the light to make him feel the full weight of his father's absence. A faraway conversation, an unexpected birthday present, a Sunday morning game of cricket in the garden ... Everywhere he turned, a long-forgotten moment played in front of his eyes.

Finally, he entered his father's study. He had spent most of last night there, sitting at the desk, writing down everything that had happened to him since he landed in Delhi. When he was done, he had placed the sheets in a manila envelope. On the outside of the envelope, he had written down Rashmi's address at *The Indian Republic*. That envelope now lay in a file folder on the desk. Tomorrow he'd mail it, and then wait and see what happened.

"Ravi."

He turned at the sound of his name to see Munje, dressed in a blue kurta-pajama, framed in the doorway.

"There was no one at the gate," Munje said, "and the front door was open."

Ravi smiled, with a shake of the head. Bahadur must have stolen away to snatch a quick cup of tea, while Hari Singh would have forgotten to lock the front door when he went to make his food. He'd have to speak to them about that.

Munje stepped into the study.

"That's what one needs today," he said, looking at the bookcase, "a good book. The only thing on T.V. is the summit. All that back and forth: What's going to happen? ... Well, anyone with an iota of common sense can see what's going to happen: *Nothing.*"

"You can't be that pessimistic," Ravi said. "Surely they'll come to some understanding."

"Not likely. India and Pakistan have a mountain of dead bodies between them; a mountain that's only grown taller since partition. It will take more than a few days of talking to get over that."

Ravi asked him to sit down. Munje settled in the chair by the desk. Ravi, for his part, was happy to remain standing.

"So how are you?" Munje asked.

Ravi shrugged his shoulders.

"I guess I'm okay," he said. "One thing's sure, though. Given what all I had to do, I didn't think anything could be worse than the last two days. Well, I was wrong. Today I feel really crappy. I just can't stop thinking of Daddy."

"That's how it usually happens, son," Munje said. "When

you lose someone, it's so much easier to deal with the world than yourself. With time, however, you will feel better."

There was a short pause. Finally, it was Munje who broke the silence.

"I must say, when I was here on Friday, I didn't realize there were so many," he said.

He gestured towards the citations hanging on the walls. Ravi, too, glanced in their direction. They covered the major portion of three walls.

"I remember when my father got the first one," Ravi said. "It was in 1979. He was running a fever that day and my mother suggested he stay home and rest and let someone else pick up the award for him. He said he would collect it himself, no matter what. 'You don't get these for a day's work, or a month's, or even a year's,' he said. 'You get these for putting in a lifetime. These are nothing short of a lifetime's wages. Surely you don't send someone else to pick up your lifetime's wages.'

"Then once he got the first one, he began to get others and ended up with so many."

"Yet in the end they didn't mean a thing to him," Munje said.

"Why do you say that?" Ravi asked.

"Well, this morning at the funeral I got talking to Dr. Verma. Or, rather, he got talking to me. I guess he was curious as to who I was. Anyway, from him I learned that your father was ill and didn't have long to live. That was why he decided to go and live with you in America. He also told me how distant you two had become and how much your father wanted to correct it towards the end of his life.

'Death, Ravi, has a way of putting things in perspective. I know that, because I am old enough to think about it myself. It forces you to see things with a clarity that's not possible otherwise. It's brutal that way, because it strips away whatever illusions you may have left.

"When your father learned he didn't have long to live, he must have come back to this room and looked at all these things that had given him so much satisfaction over the years. His lifetime's wages, as he called them. Yet at that moment, they left him cold. All he could see was how lonesome he was; so near the end of his life and yet so far away from his nearest relative.

"In that moment he realized that fame and fortune don't make up the true wages of life. It's what you earn in the hearts of people that matter to you. And looking at himself through those eyes, he saw someone who hadn't really done enough. That's why he decided to go to you in America. He was willing to give up his fame and fortune for a shot at making things right."

He wasn't the only one looking for that, Ravi thought. He sighed. If only they'd had their chance.

"What are you going to do now?" Munje asked him.

"I don't know," Ravi said. "I was so looking forward to taking my father to America. Now ..."

He shrugged his shoulders.

"Why don't you get married?" Munje said. "There's nothing like a family to fill up one's life."

"My mother was very keen on that," Ravi said. "I, however, wanted to wait until I got my green card. Before that happened, she died. I haven't thought about it since then."

He looked down. Marriage had been just one more thing that he'd put off, thinking he had all the time in the world. Before he'd known it, the time had run out. Now, after losing both his parents, he felt the lack of a family acutely.

The sound of a chair scraping on the floor made him look up. Munje was getting up.

"It's almost twelve thirty," he said, pointing to his watch. "I got so busy talking, I almost forgot the reason why I'm here.

"I came here to ask you to lunch. Or, rather, to take you. My granddaughter made it clear that I wouldn't get any lunch if I didn't bring you. Ever since she got back home from the funeral and had her bath, she's been slaving away in the kitchen. On other Sundays she'd simply fix me a snack and go off to the library. But today she's making curry, cutting vegetables, frying chappatis ... I made the mistake of thinking that all that was for me. Well, she put me wise in no time. 'God knows when that poor man last had a decent meal,' she said. 'So you'd better go and get him. And if you don't, you can forget about lunch yourself.'"

"She didn't have to go to so much trouble," Ravi began.

"Of course she didn't. But she wanted to. Now, she certainly wouldn't do it for me. But then I'm just an old Marathi man. I don't think she likes her men old or, for that matter, Marathi. I think she likes them young and Punjabi, which I guess isn't surprising. You see she takes after her mother and her mother married one of those."

His eyes were bright and the corners of his mouth were wrinkled in amusement. Ravi looked at him. Then he began to smile.